DEATHLOAD

The Highway of Destruction

By

Cy Young

"SUPERB SUSPENSE." MIDWEST BOOK REVIEW

DEATHLOAD

What if the unthinkable happened tomorrow?

BY CY YOUNG JR.

Dedication

I would like to dedicate Deathload to my son, Chuck, a man of countless talents and endless abilities. Although this work is not as deep, meaningful, or as brilliant as James Joyce's Ulysses or Finnegans Wake, it did take many hours of research and dedication to conceive, develop, and finish. I'm grateful for your example of unparalleled artistry, penetrating perception, and understanding of the unfathomable exigencies of this human experience. I'm glad to have you in my life.

DEATHLOAD

Prologue

Bursts of heavy artillery fire danced on the horizon as the staccato rumble of Saddam's big guns rolled across the windswept desert toward them. Marine Lance Corporal Vincent Fazio, Jr. squinted into the rolling clouds of dust at the road ahead.

Vincent's LAV-25 was the third Light Armored Vehicle in the convoy now highballing recklessly into heavy enemy fire. The armored unit was speeding toward Umm Hugul. The Marines were the iron fist of the thrust and Vince was beginning to get that sick feeling again in the pit of his stomach.

Operation Desert Storm was moving into high gear. Vince and his buddies had hoped the ground war would never materialize. Now reality was staring them in the face.

A shell burst off the road behind them. The LAV swerved erratically.

"Shit, that was close!" Vince's buddy yelled as he was jolted against the steel struts of the vehicle.

Norm Kleinhsauer was wishing he'd stayed at the hardware store in Monet, Missouri. It was better to be a live clerk than a dead Marine. He glanced over at his buddy.

"Hey, Vince? You scared?"

Fazio's face, illuminated in a sudden shell burst, was tense. Tense? He was scared shitless. But what the hell, he was a Marine, wasn't he?

Marines were tough assholes, square-jawed leather-necks. He could fake it as well as the next guy.

"Nah," Vince shouted, glancing at his buddy, "I saw more action last year when I visited New York!"

Norm laughed as another shell whined over-head. Both ducked as the shell went wide, bursting well to their right. Vince liked Norman. He liked most of the guys in his unit. They'd learned to stick together, be a family. Not like his own family. His father was too rich, too powerful, too busy making deals and traveling to pay much attention to him. He'd been proud when Vince joined the Marines, though. Vince knew because he'd overheard Vince Senior bragging about him to an old pal in the CIA.

Vince had mixed feelings about his dad. The man could be heartless, cruel. He'd seen him break associates, destroy them without mercy, then laugh about the way they'd squirmed and folded. Vince had learned to be tough. He'd learned from the best.

The first they knew of the Warthog was a wrenching roar behind and above them. Slow and ugly, the A-10 was one of the deadliest planes taking part in Desert Storm. The tank killer had a battery of high powered weapons which were already locking onto the convoy below. After the tragedy, the pilot swore he didn't see the markings on the LAVs identifying them as friendly. But it was war. Crazy things happened.

Norm was the first to hear the plane closing behind them and turned. "Hey, guys? We got air cover!" he shouted as he strained to see through the smoke and sand swirls erupting around them. His assumption that the plane was friendly was accurate. The Iraqi Air Force had been decimated in the first few days of the air war. Now the multi-nationals owned the air. "Go get those mothers!" he yelled at the approaching plane.

As Vince turned to look back, the A-10's two cannons fired a salvo striking the LAV and knocking it into the air. The vehicle landed on its nose with a violent thud, hop-skipping end over end half a dozen times before skidding to a stop upside down. The Marines had been blown free and were lying scattered on the sand. All except for Vincent Fazio, Jr. He was wedged under the LAV's front end, blood oozing from his mouth, his body crushed, his eyes open in a blank stare of death.

The young casualty was one of less than two hundred men killed in combat in the Gulf War. The

men who would die because of Vincent's death by
friendly fire would reach into the thousands.

....

DEATH LOAD

Phoenix Police Department 7:30 a.m. MountainTime
August 19, 1993 First Day

The Phoenix Police Department's Central Headquarters was in a modern four-story building located on palm-tree lined Washington Street in downtown Phoenix just west of the Court House. With its North and South Resource Branches, Organized Crime, Drug Enforcement and Vice Bureaus as well as a SWAT team and a Chopper unit with eight pilots, Law Enforcement in the state's capitol had come a long way.

The rugged southwest territory had been the last to yield its lawless, chaotic lifestyle. In the 1880s and 90s, the Texas Rangers were so effective that most of the outlaws fled to Arizona where law enforcement was inchoate. Desperados like Augustin Chacon, Bronco Bill, and the Black Jack Gang roamed free, robbing and killing, with just a lone sheriff and his few deputies to hold the line of law and order. A Colt .45 and nerves of steel were the only weapons of men like Sheriff John Slaughter, Capt. Harry C. Wheeler, and Col. Emilio Kosterlitzky.

Kosterlitzky, known to American troops as the "Mexican Cossack," was a colorful character who served in the Russian navy when a teenager and later in the Mexican army. Not only a rugged fighter, he was a noted linguist speaking six languages. In the early part of the 20th century, he served with the FBI as a spy for that agency.

To aid these peace officers, the Arizona Rangers was created in 1901. A paramilitary group of twenty-six men, the Rangers helped clean up the state, yank it wailing and bloody from the womb of anarchy, and usher it into the 20th century.

A precursor of the military-like structure of the modern police force, the Rangers were dissolved by the Arizona Legislature in 1909. As Phoenix grew and prospered due to the introduction of irrigation in 1911 and the railroad in 1926, the population increase brought the need for a more sophisticated law enforcement agency than the Sheriff's Office could handle. No one dreamed of just how sophisticated this new police force would become or of the unique qualities of some of the men who would make up that force.

. . . .

Detective Manny Breen hadn't been to bed in twenty-four hours. The pizza he'd wolfed at two a.m. on the stakeout felt like hot lead in his gut and the wanted felon they'd picked up had puked in the back seat of his car. Being a cop was a rotten job, and he loved it.

Due to heightened drug traffic, homicide detective Breen's eight hour shift had been increased two hours from ten p.m. to eight a.m., but the hours were a joke. He'd gone as long as five days without sleep while working on a tough case. As long as he was in the field, there was no problem. It was the paper work that slowed things down, the legal process, the muck and mire of bookings, arraignments, and court appearances. It was a pain in the ass. He resented it but it went with the job.

Manny Breen was thirty-two. He was born in Iwakuni, Japan where his father, a USMC Colonel, was stationed in 1961. Manny began studying Karate in Japan at the age of ten showing exceptional physical talent. With a black belt by age twelve, the young karate genius and kick boxer began winning tournaments and competitions, culminating with his first World Championship with the Professional Karate Association in 1977. Breen's talent: incredible speed and power. He fought with a composure and economy of movement that most fighters could not achieve.

When fighting, Manny had been described as a man whose eyes were like two bullet holes in ice.

Another physical feat adding to his exceptional abilities was achieved by a "State of Zen" technique enabling him to drop his heart rate and blood pressure dramatically. While in this state of mental stillness, he was able to hold his breath for twenty minutes.

By the time he was twenty, Manny had won more titles and become the greatest karate champion in history. He enlisted in the Marines, taught karate and kickboxing to his buddies, and was in the Gulf War in 1990. Breen left the Marines in 1991. He joined the Phoenix P.D. as a detective in early 1992 and was still winning contests.

In superb condition, he ran ten miles a day after working out for two hours, a hard feat with his demanding duties as a detective. His endurance was legendary; three days without sleep had become a staple of his work habits.

....

Breen and his partner had arrived at Central Headquarters a little before 7:30 a.m. and while Manny had escorted the suspect to the third floor to book him, Lt. Joey Payne had taken the car to be sanitized. As Breen pulled his reluctant captive past the Desk Sergeant toward a holding cell, he was thinking he'd definitely gotten the better part of the deal when the suspect, a big, tough-looking Chicano, muttered something sacrilegious in Spanish, then refused to go another step.

A street fighter trained in the martial arts, the Chicano had always been more than a match for any three men in a brawl. A few hours ago, he'd had a humbling experience.

After receiving a tip, Breen and his partner had broken in on the suspect who'd taken a room at the Camelback Inn in Scottsdale and was engaged in a sexual marathon with his favorite hooker. He'd jumped out of bed bare-assed naked ready to fight. The last thing he remembered was seeing Manny smile. He woke up an hour later with a terrible throbbing in his right temple.

"C'mon, c'mon, move it!" Breen said impatiently. The muscular, pock-marked Chicano didn't budge but stood staring defiantly at his captor through sullen, half-closed eyes.

"Fuck you!" he muttered as he tried to kick Breen in the stomach. Breen grabbed his foot and twisted. The Chicano screamed in pain, hit the ground hard, and lay there moaning. Breen looked down at him and shook his head.

"Hey, champ, you're in America now, Americans don't talk that way, do they, Sarge?"

The Desk Sergeant, who'd been on hold, was about to answer Breen when his party on the other end of the phone returned and said something the Sergeant didn't like.

"He what?" the Sergeant said in disbelief. His face flushed with anger as he shouted into the receiver. "You tell him he'd better fucking well find it, it's evidence in a fucking felony! If he fucking lost it, then he better fucking find it!" He slammed the receiver down and looked at Manny. "Do you believe this? That numb-nut asshole in Property lost 10 pounds of crack! He's not smart enough to steal it, that's why I know he lost it. Jesus!"

Manny looked at his prisoner. "He's the exception," he said, indicating the Sergeant. Breen reached down and yanked the Chicano to his feet. Holding a tight grip on his captive's arm, he forced the limping Mexican down the hall toward the squad room.

....

Bleary-eyed detectives on the 8 a.m. homicide shift were just arriving in the squad room struggling to get the left side of the brain to catch up with the right side. Strong coffee usually did the trick.

A gaunt, older detective sitting staring blankly at his typewriter looked up. A holdover from Breen's late-night shift, his eyes were bloodshot and his five o-clock shadow seemed to deepen as he spoke.

"Hey, Breen? You psychic or what? You beat the spread by one point!" He slammed the carriage return on his beat-up Smith Corona and leaned back in his chair.

"So pay up," Manny said as he shoved his prisoner again. The Chicano stopped and turned, shooting him another challenging look. Manny knew he was anxious for a second shot at him but he wasn't in the mood.

"Who misses four straight free-throws?" the older detective said with a scowl. He turned to an Asian-American detective sitting at the next desk who was helping an elderly male mugging victim look at mug shots.

"Hey, Ho? You see the game?"

"No, I was watching MacNeil Lehrer," the Asian said without cracking a smile.

The older man, Det. Pratt, shook his head and looked over at Manny who was still involved in a face-off with his suspect. "We should send this Jap back to Osaka. Who do you like on Saturday?"

"Suns by five," Manny said.

"Never happen, the Suns can't do jack-shit since McLeod left."

Det. Ho, the slightly built Asian detective, looked over his horn-rimmed glasses at a fresh-faced rookie who was observing the ritual. Ho nodded toward Pratt. "Why does he keep calling me a JAP? Isn't that a Jewish American Princess?"

The squad room erupted in laughter at the pun as Manny's partner entered carrying an antique rifle. A stocky man with a slight paunch, Joey Payne was munching a day-old prune danish. "Gun dealer in Prescott had this in a back room," Joey said, "you get this one, I'll give you a week's pay!" He threw the rifle to Manny who caught it with one hand as the older detective turned to Ho.

"Fifty bucks says he can call it," he said.

Det. Ho looked at Pratt. "I may be Jewish, but I'm not stupid."

Manny was several feet from the Chicano who was standing with his hands cuffed behind his back. As Breen dropped his eyes to examine the rifle, a cop passed them pushing a black pimp in front of him. Seizing the opportunity, the Chicano jumped high in the air, tucked his knees to his chest, and swung his cuffed hands under his feet. He landed with his hands in front of him and grabbed the cop's service revolver.

The trick had taken a split-second, but as the Chicano turned to fire, Manny broke the man's kneecap with a swift kick, then knocked him out with the butt of the rifle. As the Chicano writhed in pain on the floor, Breen casually continued his examination of the weapon.

"This looks a lot like the Mini rifle used in Europe in 1851 … but I'll go with the 1853 Pattern Enfield British Army, muzzle loading percussion rifle, 9.577 caliber…" Manny looked up. "Am I close?"

"Son-of-a —!" Joey said, his mouth hanging open. "How'd you do that?"

"Lucky guess," Manny answered as he tossed the gun back, then looked down at his groaning prisoner.

"I meant the kick, how'd you do that?"

"Beats me, Joey, my feet go crazy." Manny knelt down and yanked the moaning dealer to his feet. "Where'd you learn that trick, huh? Teach me that trick, pretty-boy!"

"Fuck you!" the Chicano mumbled as he tried to put weight on his leg, cried out in pain, and crumbled to the floor. Manny shook his head. "Your vocabulary may hurt you socially."

The rookie watched as Manny disappeared with his prisoner through the door leading to the holding cells. He turned to Det. Ho. "Pretty tough guy."

Ho looked at the rookie. "You might say that."

"What was that stuff with the rifle?"

"Manny was a gunnery sergeant in the army," Det. Ho said —-

"We keep tryin' to find a weapon he can't I.D.", Det. Pratt cut in, finishing the sentence.

"Ever happen?"

"Not yet," Pratt said, then wistfully, "but there's always a first time.

....

Plunked awkwardly in the valley between two plateaus, the flat, rectangular building stood out in garish contrast to the desert's natural beauty. Casual observers might have dismissed the structure as being nothing more than an old abandoned warehouse without stopping to wonder what it was doing in the middle of nowhere. The hidden cameras in the eaves of the building and the sensitive electronic sensors scanning the surrounding area might have been apparent to more discerning viewers, however. Those who knew what to look for.

Like the two "hikers" who left Quartzsite, a small town near I-95 and I-10 six months earlier, supposedly looking for buried treasure. They hadn't returned and no trace of them had been found.

Nearly a city block long, the building appeared to be constructed of reinforced concrete. The southerly winds whipping off the plateau had formed sand drifts against the north wall where half a dozen tumbleweeds had been halted in their journey across the desert floor by the intruding structure. As the early morning sun began to bake the building's outer shell, a rattlesnake slithered down the single set of tire tracks that led away from the building in an easterly direction.

On a crest of rocks overlooking the valley, a man stood studying the building through a pair of binoculars. His Honda Accord LX was parked on the road fifty feet below. Beside it his hand-picked squad waited in two vehicles: a black van for the dozen who would be the vanguard of the convoys and a large moving van with the words "A Moving Experience" painted on the sides containing the back-up contingent.

It was about to begin. The man could feel his heart beating more rapidly, anticipating the actual moment. He smiled at the familiar surge of adrenalin. No matter how many assignments he'd gone on in the old days at the CIA, he'd always felt this tingle of anticipation. As the nature of the assignments inured him to the danger, the feeling had grown less intense, but it was always there.

It had taken twenty-four months of mammoth effort. The energy required to accomplish each step of the project had been astounding. Only a man of his wealth and power could have done it. He'd spent half his fortune, but every cent had been worth it. The biggest problem hadn't been the gathering of data or the locating and clandestine procurement of all the necessary weapon systems. It had been the secrecy. Even those he trusted most had been carefully watched, and a number of "problem" personnel had been eliminated.

Now the period of waiting was over. All his anguish and bitterness would soon be vindicated.

"How much longer, Vince?" The man standing beside him, although tall, was a head shorter. He too was staring at the building through binoculars.

The taller man looked at his watch as the second hand approached the six. "Thirty seconds," he said. Vincent Fazio, Sr. looked back at the valley and slowly raised the binoculars.

....

The interior was the size of a football field, akin to a sprawling manufacturing plant stripped of all machinery. Numerous oil slicks stained the cement floor and a smell like sweet charcoal smoke with the hint of sulfur, indication of a propellant, along with diesel fuel, hung in the air. The only light allowed inside filtered through embrasures placed every fifty yards. These recessed openings flared outward resembling the ancient parapets of a fortification. Naked, abandoned gun mounts within the openings bore testimony to the fact that these openings were more than just an architect's flight of fancy. As for the building itself, it was empty.

Except for the two trucks.

To call them trucks was a mistake. They looked more like massive black demons from hell. Bigger than the biggest rig on the road, these burly, hulking giants possessed ominous rounded black domes that soared above the trucks' black cabs, then rounded off with sensuous curves into seamless metal bodies. Nearly two stories high, at thirty tons each, together they weighed slightly less than an Abrams M-1 Tank. This combined weight would chew up any surface structure on which the trucks traveled. It didn't matter. They would only be making one trip.

For a deathless moment, there was a hush, as if the building had just entered the eye of a hurricane. The trucks stood motionless, two predators crouched and ready to spring with savage ferocity on everything in their paths.

At precisely 7:30 a.m., as if responding to a silent command, the cab windows of both trucks rolled up with military precision; their headlights snapped on simultaneously; each souped-up 1,500 horse-power gas turbine engine turned over with an atavistic growl as an arc of electricity sparked along both bodies causing them to pulsate with a soft glow of pure energy.

Panels slid up with a hum on the sides of both trucks revealing rocket launching racks that began firing missiles at the walls and supports of the bunker. Explosions erupted all around the two killing machines as the building began to disintegrate — a two-ton metal girder slammed into one of the trucks and bounced off without leaving a scratch.

Outside, the building was now a blazing inferno spewing black smoke, and as multiple explosions continued, ripping the structure apart, the trucks emerged unscathed, then moved slowly across the desert floor toward the plateau to the north, squashing not only the charred remains of the rattlesnake but the two skulls bleaching in the sun, each with a bullet hole in the forehead.

....

On the plateau overlooking the valley, Vincent Fazio lowered the binoculars with a look of grim satisfaction.

"They're magnificent, Vincent!" the man standing beside him said in awe, "I'd never believed it was possible."

"Shows you what half a billion in small change can accomplish," Fazio said, looking at his watch. "The President should be getting his message about now. Let's get going."

At that exact moment, an unusual incident was occurring near the White House in Washington, D.C.

....

Pennsylvania Avenue near the White House
10:31 a.m. Eastern Standard Time

Ray Eisner was worried. He was being audited by the IRS and although he hadn't done anything illegal, he was afraid they'd find some way to wring more money out of him. A freelance writer, he'd claimed a number of deductions on his Schedule "C." The IRS had questioned his entertainment and phone call items and even though he had all the receipts, they could disallow some or all of the expenses.

"Damn!" he said out loud as he rounded 19th Street and headed east on Pennsylvania Avenue toward the White House, "That's all I need!"

He usually jogged before 8 a.m. but last night he'd had a fight with his wife over their disastrous financial condition. They hadn't gotten to bed until 4 a.m.

His job as a teacher of Political Science at George Washington University was not a high paying position, but it gave him plenty of time to write. Located at 19th and E, its close approximation to both the White House and his apartment was extremely convenient. With one How-To book published and another one under consideration, Ray had begun to feel his writing career was shifting, if not into high gear, then maybe into second. But his wife, a frustrated artist, kept him off balance with her mood swings. She'd been a sculptress and ... he looked toward the White House three blocks away in time to see a huge clump of multi-colored balloons. At first he thought they were tied to a slow-moving vehicle because his vision was obstructed by parked cars, but then he caught a glimpse of the clown.

Dressed in a polka dot costume, wearing floppy shoes, he was clutching two bunches of balloons in each hand.

As Ray crossed 17th Street puzzling over the clown's presence, he was surprised to see him release the balloons. Fascinated, Eisner slowed to a jog. He could see the bright multi-colored spheres through the bare tree branches as they soared toward and over the White House.

To his surprise, the balloons suddenly began softly popping open, spewing a flurry of leaflets on the lawn. Security guards appeared instantly on the roof and grounds, guns drawn, waiting for an attack to begin. None came.

Distracted by the balloons, Ray didn't see the clown hop into a car that sped away down Pennsylvania Avenue to be quickly lost in traffic. But as he crossed over to the sidewalk in front of the White House, he did catch one of the black leaflets as it zig-zagged onto the street. Printed on the narrow slip of paper were the words …

CELEBRATION

"August 21, 3:15 p.m."

....

Manny had a secret yearning. All his life he'd wanted to be a Catcher. He'd dreamed about it often but never told anyone. How would they understand? It had nothing to do with baseball. It had to do with Holden Caulfield, J.D. Salinger's hero.

Holden had been Manny's hero too ever since he'd first read the book at nine, but it wasn't a very practical thing to do: sit in a field of rye and save kids from falling over a cliff. So Manny did the next best thing. He became a Marine, which resulted in his seeing action in Operation Desert Storm. He hadn't kept anybody from falling off a cliff, but he had saved his squad when it was pinned down by enemy fire by single-handedly taking out two tanks and over 40 enemy soldiers. They'd given him a bunch of medals.

In 1992, he'd left the Marines and joined the Phoenix P.D., and as a detective, he'd already earned more commendations than anyone on the force. Ever.

....

After placing his captive in a holding cell, Manny headed back to the squad room. As he entered, he cuffed his hands behind his back. The detectives knew what was coming and jumped to their feet.

"Place your bets, boys!" Det. Pratt said as he and the others formed a circle around Breen.

Joey said, "Ten bucks says he gets it the first time!"

"You're on!"

Money slapped on the desk as Manny stood in the middle of the circle. He concentrated for a moment, then gathered himself, leapt high in the air and tried to swing his cuffed hands under his feet as the Chicano had done, but his foot caught on one of the cuffs. He went down hard.

"Aw, crap!" Joey said.

One of the guys said, "Ooo, ooo," with a sarcastic laugh as others moaned. "That must have hurt!"

Manny shrugged and got to his feet. "One more time."

Joey turned to Pratt. "Double or nothing?"

"You got it, sucker!" Pratt said laying his money on the desk.

Manny tried the trick again. This time he got one leg over and landed straddling the cuffs. "It's been a long night," he said with a sigh.

"Uh, huh," Joey said as he shuffled away, chagrined. The other detectives went back to their desks leaving Manny in an awkward, half-crouching position.

"Somebody want to unlock these?" Manny said. The men in the squad room busied themselves with paperwork. One of them stifled a giggle.

"C'mon, guys," Manny pleaded, "have a heart."

The pimp ambled over, took the keys from Manny's pocket and unlocked the cuffs.

"See? I got a heart," he said with a twisted smile.

"Thanks," Manny said, "now get your heart and your pimp ass back over there."

The pimp rolled his eyes, walked over to a chair, and sat down.

....

The squad room was relatively quiet now except for the clacking of the Telex, the hum of computers, and the clickety clack of the few old-fashioned electric typewriters left in the squad room. Det. Ho had escorted his mugging victim to the door, the rookie was off on his first tour of duty, and Det. Pratt was just finishing his investigative report.

Manny approached his desk, tore a page off his notepad with an address written on it, and stuffed it in his pocket.

"I'm out of here, guys," he said just as Joey walked through the door.

"Where you going?"

"I'm buying my little sister a new Toyota Corolla for her birthday."

Det. Pratt whistled. "What'd ya' do, rob a bank?"

"Nah," Det. Ho said, "he's on the take."

Joey lit a cigarette. "Yeah, the Chicano must have bribed him to let him go." He walked over to Det. Pratt's desk. "By the way," Joey said, "have you seen his 'little sister'?"

Det. Pratt rolled his eyes. "Yeah, five foot nine, I wish she was mine!"

"I hear she was runner-up for Miss America."

"Yeah, she should have won."

Manny stopped at the door and turned back. "I'll see you guys at my place, 6:00. Don't eat lunch, I got two tons of ribs."

Joey said, "Wait, I'll walk down with you."

"Uh, uh, we take the elevator," Manny said as they entered the hall.

Joey looked at his friend, then smiled. "Living dangerously, aren't we?"

Ever since he could remember, Manny'd had a problem with confinement in narrow places. He'd been to see a shrink or two, read several books on phobias, and understood intellectually that his fear was groundless. It didn't matter. He remembered once when he was a kid, the coach of his baseball team had taken the gang out for ice cream after a game. Manny had been the first one into the back seat, and when all the other boys had piled in on top of him, he'd panicked. The coach had pulled over and Manny, mortified but unable to control it, had gotten in the front seat with him. By the time they reached the elevator, Manny was perspiring.

....

The early morning traffic on I-10 East heading toward Phoenix had been thinning, but due to a sloppily packed pickup truck, half a dozen cardboard boxes containing books and papers had blown loose and were littered across the highway. Cars and trucks had slowed, causing a logjam while the distraught young man who was doing a friend a favor had stopped on the shoulder and was trying to retrieve what he could.

The two massive trucks were stuck just ahead of Fazio's Honda and the other two vehicles, but as the last of the debris was cleared, they started moving, at first with traffic, and then through it as they began picking up speed.

....

Elevator, Phoenix P.D.
8:40 a.m. Mountain Time

As soon as the elevator door closed, Manny knew he'd made a mistake. His breath started coming in short gasps and his whole body was covered with perspiration.

Joey looked at him anxiously. There were only four of them in the elevator. They had two levels to the main floor, but when the elevator stopped at the second floor, four detectives got on pressing Manny and Joey toward the rear of the car.

Joey saw Manny tense, then close his eyes and drop his head to his chest.

"Only one flight to go," Joey said cheerfully. One of the detectives in front of him turned back and gave Joey a funny look.

The door was taking its time closing. Joey continued breezily trying to fill the time.

"Hey, Manny? There's this sensational-looking waitress I met last night, she ..."

"Excuse me," Manny said. He pushed his way through the men to the front of the elevator and stepped out just before the door closed.

"Jeez!" one of the detectives said indignantly, "What's your hurry?"

As the elevator closed and continued to the first floor, the detective looked back again at Joey. "Was it something I said?"

"He's claustrophobic," Joey said.

"Then why'd he get in in the first place?"

"Trying to beat it."

The detective looked at the cop on his right. "Must be a lot of laughs on an airplane."

....

Phoenix was flat, dry, and hot. When Manny walked outside the main entrance onto Washington Street, the air hit him like a furnace blast. In the last few days the temperature had risen to over one hundred degrees by late morning, and it was going to be another scorcher.

Betsy's ten year-old Toyota was parked at the curb. Manny's sister, wearing a red bandanna around her hair, honked and waved when she saw Manny, then got out of the car as Joey came out of the building.

Manny met her at the curb near the front of the car. "Hi, baby," he said, giving her a kiss.

"Hi, Manny, hi Joey."

Out of deference to Manny, Joey tried hard not to look at her legs. It wasn't easy. Betsy was a tall, vivacious woman in her early twenties. Dressed in a pair of tight-fitting jeans and a simple white blouse, she was a knockout. Her short, blond hair framed high cheek bones and the bluest eyes west of the Mississippi. A man passing by in a Jaguar stared at her, nearly rear-ending a car stopped at a traffic light. Joey knew how the guy felt.

"Are you sure you want to do this?" Betsy said. "I mean, my God, a new car is absolutely astronomical today!"

"Cool it, kid, I never got you anything nice before."

Betsy looked at Joey. "Listen to this guy! He puts me through Arizona U., pays for my dancing lessons, I need a new dress he buys …"

"Yeah, yeah, yeah, let's go."

Betsy smiled. "You want to drive?"

"No, I'll follow in my car. I have to see a witness in Stanfield on a murder case. Take the exit just before Casa Grande."

"Okay." Betsy walked back around in front of her car and threw Joey a ravishing smile over her shoulder. "'Bye, Joey."

Joey waved and said, "'Bye. Hey! Pick one up for me!" He gave in to the urge and stared helplessly at Betsy's legs as she disappeared around the car.

Manny walked across the street to his Ford Mustang Coupe, made a U-turn and followed Betsy's car as she turned east on Washington heading for

I-10. He would regret his decision to take his own car for the rest of his life.

....

I-10 Eastbound
8:45 a.m. Mountain Time

Betsy Breen wasn't a good driver, but because she lived in Phoenix and everybody had a car, she'd been behind the wheel since the age of sixteen. Manny had taught her to drive, and he'd chiseled the basics into her brain through interminable repetition: hands firmly on the wheel at ten and two o'clock, check the rearview mirror every five seconds and most important, never tailgate. She'd gotten lax lately and it occurred to her as she neared the entrance to I-10 East that Manny would be pissed if he knew how she'd begun to ignore his stringent teaching.

Traffic on the freeway was light. Betsy merged easily onto I-10 and glanced in her rearview mirror. Manny was there several car lengths back. She settled into the slow lane, adjusted her seat cushion, and increased her speed to fifty-five. Ecstatic at the idea of owning a new car, she was picking up her boyfriend at Arizona University that afternoon to take him for a ride.

....

Several miles behind, the two trucks traveling south on I-17 slowed due to heavy merging traffic, then took the exit ramp leading to I-10 East.

....

Manny slid a cassette of Paul Simon's latest hits into the deck, turned the air conditioner up and settled in behind Betsy. He'd been wanting to buy her the car for over a year now but his finances hadn't allowed it. A pay hike was on the horizon and a local entrepreneur had approached him about starting a string of martial arts schools. Manny was considering it. At any rate, he felt better now about his financial future. He'd float a loan with the car dealer in Mesa. The guy had been a high school buddy; he'd give Manny a good deal.

He glanced in the rearview mirror. An Olds Sedan was keeping pace behind him in the slow lane and a Cadillac was creeping up in the fast lane. There were a few cars farther back but traffic was light. He looked ahead as Betsy waved from her Toyota. Manny waved back.

....

The two behemoths were on I-10 East now accelerating through traffic with the agility and swiftness of Jaguars as each gas turbine power plant effortlessly sucked air into its compressor, then squeezed the air in its combustion chamber causing it to expand and drive the huge turbine blades.

The amazing maneuverability of the huge vehicles was made possible by dual reduction drive bogies that evenly distributed weight over the rear axles giving them extra traction and stability.

The trucks bullied their way into the second lane forcing a Chevy van with Florida plates to brake and drop back quickly. Staying close together, the rear truck was never more than twenty feet behind its sister, never leaving space for an intruder vehicle to get between them. They were inseparable. A deadly unit. One.

....

Sharon Kramer nosed the Phoenix P.D. chopper down and dropped to an altitude of one hundred feet.

"Do you see him?"

Her partner in the chopper, Lt. Pete Field, was studying the ground below through powerful binoculars. "Not yet," he said.

The chopper had been called in to support ground units searching for a suspect in a bank robbery. The suspect, a young black man in his teens, had fled on foot after a passing squad car had thwarted the attempted hold up in northwest Phoenix. The police had lost him when their patrol car hit another vehicle at the intersection of 17th Avenue and Roosevelt.

The chopper's radio crackled with static as Sharon picked up the mic. "117CR, do you read? Come in."

"This is 117CR, go ahead."

"Do you see anything?" a male voice said urgently. One of the squad cars below had patched in to the chopper's 800 megahertz frequency.

"Negative," Sharon said as she quickly scanned the residential section below. She was about to angle the aircraft in an easterly direction when her partner's voice cut through the cabin noise.

"There he is!" Lt. Field shouted, pointing. Sharon followed his direction and saw a man running from behind a shed toward a backyard fence.

"We have the suspect in sight," Sharon said into the radio mic, "he's north of you one block, running eastward in a vacant lot on … Linden."

The radio crackled before the policeman answered. "We're on our way!"

. . . .

"We'll show you where he is," Sharon added as she put the mic on its hook and increased the rotor's thrust. The chopper responded instantly, knifing in a steep descent toward the vacant lot as the diesel's whine went up an octave.

The easy maneuverability of the aircraft amazed her. Incorporating a breakthrough design which eliminated the tail rotor, the new Notar 520 N Model was notably more maneuverable than the previous McDonnell Douglas 500 Frame chopper but gave a quieter, smoother ride. A lot different than the heavier Sikorsky HH-3E she'd flown with the 101st Airborne. One of only twenty-two women to pilot helicopters in Desert Storm, Sharon's job had been to ferry ammo and supplies to the troops advancing on Saddam's Republican Guard. She'd nearly been killed when her Sikorsky had come perilously close to a power line in the darkness. It was only after landing that she realized how close she'd been to death.

The only woman among eight police department chopper pilots, Sharon had undergone the usual male kidding about her position in a traditionally male-oriented job. She didn't mind. Sharon wore men well, enjoyed their company and was able to diffuse any hostility with her offhand charm and ready laugh. Her ease with the opposite sex probably was due in great part to her three older brothers.

What she went through now with men was gravy compared to the roughhousing she'd been subjected to while growing up with her athletic siblings. She was grateful for it though … it prepared her for the male-dominated world she was going to have to survive in.

In less than twenty seconds, the chopper reached the fleeing suspect and hovered over him as he ran into another vacant lot. Confused and frightened, he looked up at the chopper, then disappeared into a clump of bushes.

. . . .

Manny estimated he was ten car lengths behind Betsy. It was a safe distance, allowing him plenty of time to stop if something happened on the road ahead, yet it was close enough to keep Betsy's car in view. As he passed a merging ramp, a Dodge Dart entered the freeway ahead of him, but before he could pass the car, it knifed over to the fast lane and sped away.

Casa Grande was another ten miles. He glanced at his watch, figuring the time it would take to help Betsy wrap up the sale. Manny wanted to get to Stanfield by eleven o'clock. The man he was interviewing was an employee at a 7-Eleven store where a robbery/slaying had occurred last month. The owner had been shot dead by two men wearing stocking caps. Their M.O. was to hit after midnight, force everyone to lie down, then empty the cash register. The shorter of the two would then take several bags of potato chips and Baby Ruth candy bars. Homicide had nicknamed them the Junk Food Gang.

The other two witnesses were a husband and wife from Tucson who had been customers in the store when it was hit. Manny wanted to see them next and wrap up the first part of the investigation. He had to be in court on another homicide case at two o'clock. Barring unforeseen hangups, he should make it.

Breen looked out across the irrigated plains of the Salt River Valley. The gently rolling desert terrain of Maricopa County was spotted with stands of giant saguaro cactus which grew only in southern Arizona, Colorado, and the state of Sonora, Mexico. Manny was familiar with the tall, stately cacti. He'd found a body buried under one.

A billboard announcing the all-Indian rodeo that took place each August popped into view on his right. The rodeo was the highlight of a powwow honoring the area's ancient inhabitants, the Hohokam, Papago, Maricopa and Apache cultures that had occupied the Gila River Basin for over two thousand years. He'd gone to one a few years ago where he'd met an Apache who was competing in some of the events. They'd become good friends and Manny had helped him get on the police force. Now a detective assigned to the Burglary and Theft Division at the North Resource Bureau, Dan Lightfoot had turned into that department's best cop.

A sign reading CASA GRANDE FOUR MILES brought Manny back to reality. Betsy's car was still sitting ten car lengths in front of him. He glanced in his rearview mirror. I-10 curved gently to the southeast at this point giving him a sweeping view of the road behind him. Traffic was light except for two trucks several miles back.

....

"They're going too fucking fast!" Vincent Fazio glanced at his speedometer hovering around seventy-two. He was trying to stay with the trucks, but they kept pulling away. He glanced in his rearview mirror. The van and moving van were trailing behind him as planned, but the excessive speed of the trucks could call attention to the convoy, put the highway patrol on their tail and jeopardize the operation. It's true the trucks were the nearest thing to being invulnerable, but there was always the chance something could go wrong.

"Asians are notoriously bad drivers," the man sitting next to Fazio said with a smile. "Oshiba programmed the trucks; eighty is his average speed. I drove with him once from New York to D.C. in his souped-up Porsche. My heart was in my mouth the whole time. He hit one-fifty. Said he wanted to see how good his mechanic was."

"And nobody stopped you?"

"He had all kinds of radar and jamming devices, something similar to the way the trucks are set up. Always knew when the police were around, then he'd slow down."

"He's a smug asshole," Fazio said, "nobody can tell him anything."

"He's a genius, what else do you expect?"

"As far as computers go he is, but when it comes to strategy, he's an idiot."

"Relax, Vincent, the trucks can take care of themselves. If a patrol car tries to stop them, you know what'll happen.

Fazio looked at John Jamington Fryer, head of the CIA's Counter-terrorism Division. Fryer's red hair was thinning and brown spots around his temples were becoming more obvious. He'd always reminded Fazio of a thin Red Skelton, except that Fryer was no comedian. He was the CIA's expert on communications and had been instrumental in the development and deployment of the KH-11 spy satellite program. A valuable tool in Fazio's plan for revenge, Fryer, nicknamed J.J., had worked closely with Oshiba in the early stages of the project. He'd supplied the Asian with the terrain maps needed to program the trucks to operate on their own with no risk of human failure. Without his help, the plan wouldn't have been possible. But now he was bugging Fazio.

"Nobody seems to understand," Fazio said, measuring his words, "how intense my feelings are about this project. This is not just another assignment for me, J.J., this is fucking life and death!"

J.J. started to interrupt but glanced at Fazio's face. He decided it was better to hold his peace. Fazio continued.

"This is just a diversion for you. It gives you a chance to get away from the insane paranoia that goes with your job. For Oshiba it's fun; he loves fucking around with computers. But I've got this thing inside me, it's eating my guts out! Every day I see Vinnie's face, I remember things we did, his first birthday party when he was two, his first day at kindergarten, the first football game I took him to …"

Fazio's voice trailed off as he wandered through his storehouse of memories.

J.J. stared straight ahead. *Why doesn't he get past this*, he thought. *Everybody loses somebody, why is he so hung up on his son?*

He already knew the answer. It was Fazio's ego. That's what this was all about. It had little to do with Vincent Jr.'s death; it had to do with his father's incredible ego. They'd done something to *him*, not his son. J.J. smiled. Maybe that was the reason Fazio had been such a successful field operative during his tenure with the CIA. He'd survived many times where lesser men would have been eliminated. *So let him have his ego,* J.J. thought. *It's a better indul-gence than grief for a dead son or getting killed by some asshole double agent with a poison-tipped um-brella.*

He glanced down at the scar on his hand. He'd gotten it during the CIA-backed war in Laos when the CH-3 Jolly Green Giant chopper he'd been flying on a search and rescue operation had been hit by en-emy fire and gone down near Phou Pha Thi. Fazio had flown in with a few men, killed dozens of VC surrounding the downed chopper, and saved his life. He owed Vincent … and today was payday.

....

Because Betsy Breen had had a hectic morning, she was doing something she shouldn't have been doing while driving a car down the freeway at fifty-five mph.

A stewardess with Southwest Airlines, she'd touched down the night before from her L.A. flight at 8 p.m. Steve had met her at Sky Harbor International Airport, they'd had a quick bite to eat, then gone back to her apartment in Scottsdale where they'd watched the classic movie "Laura" on Betsy's VCR. They'd made love longer than Betsy would like to admit and hadn't gotten to sleep until after four that morning. She'd jogged at six, gone back to bed for another half hour, driven Steve to A.U. where he was teaching a class in English Lit., and had just made it to Police Headquarters in time to meet Manny a little before nine. She hadn't had time to put on her makeup. That's why she was looking in the mirror now and applying eye shadow between glances at the traffic ahead.

Her makeup kit was open beside her on the seat. She finished the eye shadow, then fished around in the kit while inspecting her face. Her fingers found her favorite eyebrow pencil. She pulled the plastic cover off with her teeth and started on her eyes. The damn pencil was dull. Betsy cursed under her breath but did the best she could. She thought about waiting until after buying the car, but she hated to be seen without her makeup. There'd probably be a bunch of guys at the dealership and who knows? Maybe some of them would be potentials. She had to be ready.

Betsy glanced in the sideview mirror. Manny's car was still there. Hoping he couldn't tell what she was doing, she applied her lipstick, blotted it with a Kleenex and tossed the used tissue on the seat beside her. It was Tuesday, her day off. She had a class at A.U. at one o'clock where she was working on her B.A. in Business Administration. Then she was going to the airport to meet a friend who was flying in from New York to spend the week. It would be a busy day. Betsy glanced at the speedometer. Her speed had increased to over sixty and she realized her foot had been holding the accelerator on the floor. She eased up until the gauge read fifty-five.

....

Manny pressed on the accelerator to maintain his speed. I-10 had begun its gradual ascent from Phoenix toward the little Dragoon Mountains near the historic town of Tombstone forty miles to the east. The Mustang was handling the upgrade well. He glanced in his rearview mirror, then moved to the second lane to pass a slow-moving A&P truck in the right lane. Betsy had already made the change; he followed her Toyota as they scooted by the truck.

The area between Phoenix and Tucson was well-populated. Numerous fast food chains had popped up just off of I-10 along with motels, gas stations, and the usual franchise restaurants. The surrounding area had seen a heavy influx of tourists, one of Arizona's biggest industries. Here I-10 passed through the Gila River Indian Reservation while a few miles to the east was the Casa Grande Ruins National Monument. Further east of Tucson were sections of the Coronado National Forest which offered a variety of terrain from rugged wooded mountains to arid desert.

One of the most popular tourist attractions was the Tombstone National Historic site with its Boothill Graveyard and O.K. Corral where Wyatt Earp shot it out with the Clanton gang. Manny hadn't seen any of these places. He'd been too busy living his life, jogging, working out, being a cop.

Still in the second lane, he checked his mirror again and noticed two trucks moving up fast in the slow lane not a mile behind. He realized they were the same vehicles he'd seen a few moments earlier. The thought occurred to him that they were traveling too fast. He hated these mammoth trucks hogging the road, speeding around like sports cars, scaring the hell out of motorists in vehicles a tenth their size. And now the trucking industry was lobbying Washington for the right to build even bigger rigs with even more capacity so they could hog even more of the road. Everything came down to money, more and more money.

A road sign ahead read CASA GRANDE 2 MILES. They were approaching the A&P truck but Betsy was still in the second lane. As he moved past the truck, Manny could see why. There was a slow-moving Pontiac in the far right lane and an Audi in front of Betsy's Toyota going around fifty-five. She was pinned in.

....

Betsy had also seen the exit sign but felt trapped. Entering and exiting highways had always been a problem for her. She'd stayed off the freeway for a whole year only driving on surface streets. Two weeks ago she'd decided her fears were silly and determined to beat them … she'd ventured out onto I-10 for a short distance slowly increasing her driving time each day. She'd begun to feel better about it … but now she was getting that panicky feeling again. She glanced in her rearview mirror. The fast lane was free but it was for crazies, the hotshots in their souped up Porsches and 300 ZXs, especially out here in the desert. But she had to make a move or they'd miss the exit.

·········

Manny had an uneasy feeling. Betsy lacked confidence; sometimes acting spontaneously was the difference between life and death. He glanced quickly in his rearview mirror. The trucks were in his lane coming up fast behind him. Too fast.

"Damn!" Manny swore as he realized he was boxed in. A second glance told him that unless he moved quickly, the front truck would rear end him in a matter of seconds. "What's the matter with that asshole?" he said out loud. Manny sped ahead until he was on Betsy's tail, honked, and when she looked in the mirror, motioned urgently for her to make a move.

Betsy saw her brother and heard him honk but she couldn't think. Her worst fears were being realized. In a blind panic, she pounded on the car horn at the Audi two car lengths ahead but it didn't budge. The Pontiac was still sitting on her right in the slow lane. She slammed her palm on the horn and kept it there as perspiration ran down her forehead and trickled mascara into her eyes, stinging them.

The guy in the Audi was from Brooklyn. He knew how to handle an aggressive son-of-a-bitch giving him a hard time. He looked in his rearview mirror, jammed his middle finger in the air and hit the brakes hard as he yelled, "FUCK YOU, ASS-HOLE!"

His move had the desired effect. He saw the broad in the Toyota behind him slam on her brakes. He floored the accelerator to avoid being rear ended, kept the pedal down and shot away, quickly reaching a speed of eighty.

As Betsy jammed on her brakes, Manny, close behind her, was forced to brake, then knife into the slow lane to avoid being rear ended by the truck.

Narrowly missing the Pontiac's rear bumper, his Mustang fishtailed, then righted itself as Manny slowed the car's swerving momentum and looked to his left as the biggest, meanest-looking truck he'd ever seen shot past him in the second lane and slammed into Betsy's Toyota. The tiny automobile burst into flames, flew through the air like a flaming torch, and hit the ground just off the shoulder where it exploded on impact.

Manny went blank. The next thing he knew he was standing on the shoulder of the road trying to get to Betsy's car but something was holding him back. He turned to see a large black man standing behind him, dragging him away from the fiery mass.

"It could explode again, you gotta …"

Before he could finish, Manny yanked free and tried to penetrate the wall of heat that was more powerful than any combatant he'd ever faced. He fell to his knees as he felt the powerful hands again pulling him to safety.

"There's nothin' you can do, buddy," the truck driver said, "it's all over!"

Manny shook his head but the nightmare wouldn't go away. "Did they stop? Did those fuckers STOP?"

The trucker looked down the highway at the disappearing behemoths. "Uh, uh," he said, "they're still goin'." His own A&P vehicle was parked on the shoulder. "I never seen two trucks move so fast on the upgrade." He looked back at Manny. "You get the license?"

Breen didn't answer, he was up and running. "Call the highway patrol!" he yelled over his shoulder as he reached his car.

Traffic was piling up behind the wreck of Betsy's car as motorists stopped to gawk at the tragic scene. Manny sped down the shoulder, found an opening, shot onto the freeway, slammed a bubble on the roof outside the car, and cut over to the fast lane nearly side-swiping a white Dodge Dart. Manny, driving a stick shift, down-shifted to third and floored the accelerator, throwing the engine into overdrive.

The trucks were nowhere in sight. Manny whipped the car around a Volkswagen Bug, veered sharply into the second lane, cut between a Jeep and a Chevy van and careened into the slow lane. He sped toward a slight rise in the road, reached it and was greeted with a sweeping view of straight pavement stretching at a gentle upgrade as far as the eye could see.

Signs of roadside civilization had thinned out. Stands of mesquite bordered the highway while to the east, Black Mountain rose above the irrigated plains of the Salt River Valley. But Manny didn't notice. He was squinting at the two black monoliths five miles ahead racing like huge mobile caskets into the brilliant morning sun. He jammed the pedal to the floor. The Mustang had just been tuned and the 351-cubic-inch motor with a four-barrel carb gave plenty of torque. It responded with a roar as the RPM needle shot across the dial and the car surged forward quickly reaching a speed of one hundred.

Traffic was increasing slightly as I-10 approached the interchange with I-8. Manny slalomed, changing lanes erratically in a zig-zag course as he closed on the trucks now in the center lane. He'd pushed the thought of Betsy out of his mind, *don't think about her now, there's only one objective, stop the fucking trucks if I have to kill the drivers to do it!* The image of Betsy's car flying though the air in flames flashed across his mind. He forced it away again focusing harder on the rear truck which was now two miles ahead.

Suddenly all three lanes closed as merging traffic from the town of Eloy flooded the freeway.

"Shit!" Manny shouted out loud as he hit the brake hard, fishtailed, then swerved sharply over onto the right shoulder, floored the accelerator and shot by the slower moving traffic quickly approaching one hundred again. He was scanning the road for the trucks when his eye caught a glimpse of the highway repair vehicle parked less than fifty yards ahead on the shoulder directly in front of him.

"Son of a Bitch!" he muttered. Without thinking, Manny swerved to the right, jumped the shoulder barely missing the repair truck, and hit a patch of blacktop still in place from the old highway. He swerved back onto the berm, saw an opening, knifed over to the fast lane and found a corridor of empty space.

The trucks were still in the middle lane, barrel-assing east, *running scared*, Manny thought. *If they get caught, their licenses will be revoked, they'll face manslaughter charges and leaving the scene of an accident!*

As Manny closed on the trucks in the fast lane, a guy in a Lumina Z34 saw him coming and cut over to the middle lane to let him pass. As Manny shot by, the highway ahead opened up leaving only the two trucks on the road. They were less than a mile away now as the Mustang ate up the distance, placing Manny within two hundred yards of the rear truck in a matter of seconds. He could see the North Carolina plates on the vehicle which read HAA-251.

Still in the fast lane, Many came up fast behind the rear truck now in the middle lane. With horn blaring, he pulled level with the rear truck's high-domed black cab. Leaning over toward the window on the passenger side, he tried to see up into the truck's cab but the windows were tinted black. "Pull over you son-of-a-bitch!" he yelled over the high-pitched scream of the truck's tires on the pavement and the raucous blast of his own horn. There was no response.

Cursing again, Manny spurted past the rear truck to the lead vehicle in the middle lane and pulled level with the cab. Again, his effort to get the driver's attention was negative. *What do I have to do,* Manny thought, *shoot these assholes to get their attention?*

Manny was demanding a lot of the Mustang. He'd never kept it at such high speed for this long; the engine was overheating badly but he had no choice. He coaxed more pull from the engine. Still in the fast lane, he passed the lead truck and swerved violently into the middle lane in front of it. He rolled his window down, waved to get the driver's attention and jabbed his finger toward the shoulder. Nothing. Manny glanced at his speedometer. He was hovering now between one hundred ten and one hundred twelve mph, the engine dangerously hot.

He snapped the heater on and turned it up high. When he looked back into the rearview mirror, the lead truck was less than ten feet behind him and closing fast. *The fucker's trying to ram me,* Manny thought! *The son-of-a-bitch is actually trying to —-*

"They're insane, they're fucking INSANE!" he shouted as he pushed the Mustang to the limit. The truck was not only gaining on him but now the second truck was pulling up fast in the far left lane. It drew alongside its sister which had moved over and was straddling the first two lanes leaving Manny no place to go but straight ahead. He realized they were trying to kill him. He knew they weren't ordinary trucks an instant later when he saw an electric current arc back and forth between the front of the two cabs.

The Mustang's speedometer was quivering at a hundred twenty. Cars on the road ahead, aware of the juggernaughts approaching at blinding speed, were scattering onto the shoulder like cockroaches caught in a sudden glare.

"Jesus!" Manny swore. The trucks were looming up behind him like killer whales about to devour a baby seal. Waiting until the last second, just before impact, he jerked the wheel hard right, shot across to the far right lane with tires screaming onto the shoulder, then yanked the wheel left and hit the brakes. The car skidded, tires smoking, as the blast of hot air from the trucks whipping by blew the car off the shoulder. Manny struggled to hold the wheel as the Mustang jumped and shimmied violently, plowing into dirt, then sand, power sliding sideways as it hit a rock and leaped in the air, then, still going sixty, sliced back across the freeway almost losing control and slamming into oncoming traffic on I-10 West.

The car's heater, combined with the desert temperature, was becoming unbearable but having the desired effect, lowering the temperature of the engine a few degrees. Manny left the heater on, yanked his 9 mm gun from its holster and floored the accelerator as perspiration running down his forehead washed sweat into his eyes.

The trucks, now in the middle lane, had slowed, one falling in behind the other. Manny caught up with them quickly this time and as he closed to within a distance of fifty yards, positioned the car in the slow lane to give himself a shot at the truck's tires.

He'd approached to within thirty yards when a brilliant flash blinded him. Manny took his foot off the accelerator, squinted, and fought away sun spots dancing in the blackness. He held the car steady until his vision began returning. The trucks had pulled away and as Manny accelerated toward them, another blinding flash rendered him helpless.

This time Manny hit the brakes on reflex sending the car careening into a sideways skid across the freeway where it bounded off the shoulder into soft sand, zig-zagged as he lost control, then overturned once and miraculously righted itself, coming to an abrupt stop in a stand of mesquite.

Dust rose around the car and settled gently over it like a thin coating of gold sparkling in the sun. All was still except for a jackrabbit that skittered away through the underbrush. After a moment, the door opened slowly. Manny rolled out onto a patch of sand, stayed on his knees a moment, stunned, got slowly to his feet and waited for his head to clear. Struggling back to consciousness, he climbed back inside the car, tried repeatedly to start it with no success as he watched the trucks diminish to two specks and disappear around a curve of the highway.

"Son of a BITCH!" he shouted, then jumped out of the car and slammed the door hard.

Traffic was backed up as far as Sacaton with drivers standing on top of their cars trying to see the cause of the hang-up. The highway at the accident scene was relatively clear of wreckage except for a mangled car door jutting partially onto the slow lane. The smoldering shell that had been Betsy's car was lying upside down just off the shoulder, the contents of her makeup kit scattered over the gravel nearby. Two truckers were spraying the wreck with fire extinguishers as three Department of Public Safety cars sped up on the shoulder, lights blinking, sirens wailing.

DPS Lt. Kaufman slammed on his brakes, skidded to a stop and swore under his breath when he saw the gutted car. The other two DPS cars pulled up, two deputies got out and walked over as Lt. Kaufman opened his door.

"Okay, Bobby," he said to the shorter man, "let's block off the right lane, clear traffic off and set up the flares about two hundred yards back."

"Right," the shorter man said, went back to his car, took out a number of flares and started walking back down the road.

"Git this traffic movin', Kevin," Lt. Kaufman said to the second deputy, "I'll do the dirty work."

The second Deputy glanced at the wreck and shook his head. "Life sucks,"he said with a sigh, then stepped onto the freeway and began directing traffic.

Lt. Kaufman got out and stepped around his car. He was starting across the gravel toward the wreck when he saw the makeup kit, stopped and stared at it. *Women didn't have the sense God gave animals and little children*, he thought. He'd seen a number of accidents where women had been making up while driving. His department had even included a segment on the dangers of that particular activity when they'd made a DPS special film on safe driving. The film had been shown several times on their local public service TV channel. *Too damn bad she hadn't seen it,* he thought as he stepped over the kit and walked up to the two truckers.

"She still in there?" he said.

The trucker with the A&P truck glanced at him. "Yeah, she's in there, what's left of her."

"Thanks for puttin' out the fire, boys, you saved our fire department some S&L."

"What's that?" The other trucker said as he turned off his extinguisher.

"Sweat and Labor," Lt. Kaufman said with a smile as he took out his writing pad. "Okay, who saw what?"

Air Space over Northwest Phoenix
9:25 a.m. Mountain Time

Sharon Kramer's chopper was hovering over the street by the vacant lot as detectives from the robbery detail, having surrounded the suspect, were yelling for him to surrender. A kid around sixteen, he kept yelling he'd shoot anyone who tried to take him, but a detective from the Special Assignments Unit was talking him out of it.

The SAU had a good record, their principal weapon being psychology, a few calm, well-chosen words, and common sense. The kid was crouched down behind a clump of bushes, scared shitless. It could've gone either way, but as Sharon and Pete watched the drama unfolding below them, they saw the kid drop his weapon, thrust his arms in the air and stand up. *Bloodshed, thank God, would be spared, at least this time,* Sharon thought.

"It's all over," she said to Pete as she picked up the radio mic. "117CR to dispatch, do you read?"

The dispatcher's voice came through loud and clear. "Go ahead, 117CR."

"Ground units have the suspect under control, no shots were fired, we got away clean on this one."

"Good show, guys."

"Shall we come in? I need to refuel," Sharon said, still watching the action on the ground as four detectives moved up to the kid and cuffed his hands behind his back. *One of the detectives would be reading him his rights about now,* she thought. The radio crackled with static before the dispatcher answered.

"Okay, but there's been an accident on I-10 just east of Casa Grande. There's a fully fueled chopper waiting at our port, you can use that. You better get over there and check it out."

"Any casualties?"

"One, we think."

"Roger, on the way."

Sharon stuck her arm out the open door and waved to the ground units who waved back as Petie slipped the safety catch of his AK-47 assault rifle back on and placed the weapon on the floor behind them.

"Never a dull moment, huh?"

"Not today anyway," Sharon said as she smiled, then nosed the chopper around, increased the rotar's thrust, and headed to the chopper pad.

....

I-10 East at the Scene of the Accident
9:30 a.m. Mountain Time

The deputy handling traffic control waved the Honda with the two men inside into the second lane. As the Honda passed, the man on the passenger side rolled his window down.

"What happened, officer?"

"Hit and run," the deputy said.

"Who did the hitting?"

"We think it was a truck, keep it moving."

"Right. Thanks, officer," the man said as he rolled the window back up.

The Honda merged into the second lane, then picked up speed. Inside the car, J.J. glanced at Fazio. "The trucks must be in defensive mode by now. We'll catch up with 'em at the next coordinate."

Fazio's face was implacable but J.J. knew he was furious.

"I'm going to call that fucking Jap! He has to make an adjustment. I don't want anymore of these screwups."

The Honda was approaching the accident scene. J.J. glanced over at the smoking hulk but Fazio kept his eyes straight ahead. This was just the first of many casualties. He hadn't planned for civilians to get hurt, but if they got in the way, so be it. He checked the rearview mirror. The black van was there and as he watched, the moving van fell in behind it. His convoy was intact. Soon, just outside Tucson, they'd be passing Luke Air Force Base, the truck's first target. But because it was near the city and there would be too much traffic, the trucks would wait until they were past Tucson, pull off on a deserted desert road and hit Luke and Davis Mon-than simultaneously. Fazio smiled in anticipation.

As the Honda picked up speed, a DPS car sped toward them going against traffic on the shoulder with two men inside.

....

The trooper in the DPS car had responded to reports of a second accident twenty miles to the east of the wipeout near Casa Grande. He'd found homi-cide detective Manny Breen walking on the shoulder, his face filled with blood from a nasty gash on the forehead. His eyes had a funny look, like he'd been crying.

Now as they drew alongside the wreck and stopped, the deputy got out but Manny stayed inside, looking through the window at Betsy's car. It still hadn't registered. Like when his mother died. He hadn't believed it for months, kept expecting her to be there when he got home from school with a cheery "Hi!" and a great dinner on the table. It final-ly got through to him on his tenth birthday six months after she'd died from an obscure virus. His parents would always take him to a fancy restaurant and let him order what he wanted.

But on his tenth birthday, she wasn't there. His dad had taken him anyway. Betsy had gone along with them. Two year old Betsy with golden curls and entrancing eyes, and now they both were gone.

He looked away from the smoking shell as two deputies working with the truckers tried to pry the door open. Manny found himself looking at his hands. They were blackened from trying to fight through the flames … and they were shaking. With all his training, all his expertise in the martial arts, his hands had been helpless in trying to save his sister. The fragility of human life hit him like a karate kick to the mid-section. With great effort he pushed the yawning chasm of grief and despair away again.

He had something to do now. Mourning would come later.

....

After switching choppers, Sharon and her partner had begun to see the congested traffic as soon as the chopper left Phoenix. Now, as they approached the scene of the accident, it was beginning to move. Then they saw the demolished car.

"My God," Pete said,"someone was actually in that thing!"

"Yeah." Sharon tried not to think about it as she positioned the chopper in the desert near the right shoulder a short distance from a DPS car. The chopper settled in, kicking up dust, and touched down. The whine of the turbine began to drop.

Manny had been standing a short distance from the wreck giving a description of the trucks to one of the deputies. He hadn't mentioned the blinding flashes. He couldn't explain it and until he could, he would wait. He was just finishing when he heard the police chopper approaching.

"Okay," the deputy said, writing a few last words in his notepad, "I'll call it in."

As the deputy turned and started back to his squad car, Manny was running toward the chopper. He approached just as Pete hopped out.

"Breen, Homicide Division!" Manny shouted flashing his badge to Pete. "I saw the accident!"

Pete stuck his head back in the chopper and yelled over the whine of the turbine. "Sharon, this is Det. Breen, he can I.D. the hit and run vehicle. I'll stay here and see if I can help out."

"Roger," Sharon shouted as Manny climbed into the seat beside her. She did a quick check of the instrument panel, brought up the revs of the turbine and increased the rotor thrust. The chopper shud-

dered, then lifted off, swiveled and headed east, flying low over the highway.

....

The trucks had slowed and were now averaging close to sixty mph as the computers corrected the error. Oshiba hadn't programmed them at too high a speed; there'd been a minor malfunction in one of the transistor connections. Built-in safety features had analyzed the problem and come up with the solution rerouting the electrical current and closing down the malfunctioning unit.

The trucks were single file traveling in the slow lane. A Chrysler Le Baron was riding several car lengths ahead of the lead truck one lane over in the middle lane.

The Stokes family from Stockton, California was headed for El Paso to visit Mrs. Stokes' mother, who was in her upper eighties. Mr. and Mrs. Stokes were in the front seat, the two children in the back seat. Jimmy, aged seven, had just snatched his toy truck away from his three-year old sister who had begun to wail.

Jimmy's mother had scolded him for not sharing, he'd given it back and also started crying.

His little sister had finally tired of playing with the truck and dropped it in the seat. She was busy now sucking her thumb and being lulled to sleep by the gentle rocking motion of the car. Jimmy had peeked over at her as his sobs subsided, seen his opportunity, and snatched the truck back. Now he was pushing it across the Chrysler's vinyl backseat, moving it faster and faster. With a quick move, he changed course and maneuvered the truck over his legs with a gurgling sound reminiscent of a car's engine and pushed the toy up the back of the seat. He stood up and was moving the truck in a zig-zag course along the top of the seat and back into the narrow flat space by the rear window when he looked out and saw a strange sight.

Just behind his dad's car, a real truck was doing funny things. The license plate had just flipped over and a fine mist was shooting out of little nozzles on the front of the truck. The mist was changing the color of the license plates from black to blood rust.

As Jimmy watched, fascinated, the lettering on the truck's side flipped over changing the words Roberts Manufacturing Co., Inc. to read United Fruit Company.

An excited Jimmy tried to tell his parents what he'd just seen but they misunderstood, thinking he was talking about his own toy truck. It didn't help that Jimmy stuttered when he was excited, and he was very excited now, stumbling over his words in a frustrated effort to make his parents understand that he was talking about the *real* truck behind them and to the left, the one that was now exiting I-10 and taking I-19.

Finally, Jimmy tired of trying to make his parents understand, sat back down, and continued rolling his toy truck across the seat of the Chrysler. He hadn't seen the same metamorphosis occurring to the second truck and wasn't aware that it was staying on I-10, splitting up with its sister.

....

The Notar was traveling at a speed close to one hundred thirty knots as it skimmed above the highway. With a one hundred fifteen gallon fuel capacity stored in two baffled fuel bladders in the belly section, the chopper could stay in the air for hours.

Both occupants were preoccupied, one with safely navigating the new, expensive McDonnell Douglas aircraft and the other one with a minute observation of everything traveling on the road below. Sharon glanced over at the detective sitting next to her. He was perspiring heavily even though it was relatively cool in the cabin.

"You saw the accident?" she shouted over the turbine's high-pitched whine.

"Yes," Manny shouted back. He was peering down at the road through binoculars.

"Hear there was a fatality," Sharon said, straining her voice. When Breen didn't answer, she thought it was because of the cabin noise. She tapped him on the shoulder and indicated a headset hanging near the seat. Manny put it on as Sharon repeated her statement into the headphones. Breen still didn't answer but went back to staring at the road.

"Take it lower," he said as he wiped the sweat away. Manny's fury at the truck drivers had outweighed his claustrophobia and forced him into the chopper. The anger still dominated, but the fear of close confinement was there, lurking inside, waiting to reach up and yank him into the blackness.

Sharon dropped the chopper until it was hovering not more than fifty feet above the freeway. Manny forced himself to focus on the road. The chopper was fast approaching a large truck. He checked the Oregon plates, then studied a truck directly in front of it with Wisconsin plates. As he was thinking these trucks were too small anyway, the chopper's radio crackled and the dispatcher's voice came on.

"Dispatch to 117CR ... do you read?"

Sharon picked up the radio mic. "Roger that, dispatch, this is 117CR. Go ahead."

"Where are you, Sharon?"

Sharon looked to her left. "Over I-10 in west Tucson near the West Congress Street exit ... close to Valencia Road ... the Flandrau Planetarium's on my left, St. Mary's Hospital on my right. We're in pursuit of that hit and run vehicle, license plate Harry Alpha Alpha 251 ..."

"I've got something on that ... hold on ..." There was a sustained silence as the dispatcher went away and returned in a moment. "Hello, 117CR ... that plate's a negative, the number didn't come up on our search."

Breen dropped the binoculars and looked at Sharon. "Let me talk to her."

Sharon handed the mic to Manny who was not only perspiring heavily but appeared to be agitated, distracted.

"This is Manny Breen, Phoenix Homicide Division. I I.D.'d that plate number, what do you mean it didn't turn up?"

A beat as the dispatcher checked her information. "Sorry," the scratchy voice said, "that's still a negative."

Breen's face flushed. "I know what I saw," he shouted into the mic,"I know what I FUCKING SAW!"

"Well, *excuse me——!*" The dispatcher said as Manny shoved the mic back to Sharon. She noticed his hand was shaking.

"You okay?" Sharon said, watching him closely.

"No!" he shouted as he focused his attention again on the traffic below, "I'm NOT fucking okay!"

Sharon studied Manny for a moment before speaking into the mic.

"Let me know if anything turns up," she said. "Ten four."

"Ten four."

·········

Sharon placed the mic back on its hook and was about to say something when the delicate balance between Breen's anger and his fear inclined suddenly toward fear. He exploded.

"TAKE IT DOWN!" he shouted.

"What?" Sharon answered, startled by the intensity of his voice.

"TAKE IT DOWN!" he repeated in panic, "I HAVE TO GET OUT!"

"Are you sick?"

"What?" Manny said.

"ARE YOU SICK?"

"Yeah, I'm sick, TAKE IT DOWN!"

Sharon spied a lip off the shoulder reserved for disabled vehicles and settled on it. The instant the chopper touched down, Breen lurched out of the chopper onto the pavement. He gulped air and began hyperventilating. After a moment, he reentered the chopper. The look of panic had subsided, but his face was a mess. There was a large bump on his forehead and a gash over his eyebrow was oozing blood down the side of his cheek.

"I've got a paper sack in back if you …"

"No, it's okay," Manny said impatiently, let's go, let's go!"

Sharon didn't move. She stared at him as the thump, thump of the rotors rocked the aircraft with a soft, rhythmic motion.

Breen stared back at her. "What are you waiting for, let's go!"

"You look sick to me, and by the way, how'd you hurt your head?"

"It's a bump I got chasing the trucks, okay? Can we go now?"

"Just a bump? It's the size of a goose egg, you should've had the EMS people look at it."

"It's not the size of a goose egg!" Breen shouted back.

"Yes, it is," Sharon insisted. She was trying to get him to chill out but he wasn't buying it.

Breen was furious. His eyes leveled on her with the deadliness of a cobra about to strike. "Have you seen a goose egg? HAVE YOU EVER SEEN A REAL FUCKING GOOSE EGG?" he shouted.

Sharon thought a moment. "I must have," she said thoughtfully, "but not recently."

Manny stared at her a moment, then said, "Can we stop discussing my bump and go after the trucks? *Please?*" He ran his fingers through his thick, black hair with a quick movement. His eyes focused on Sharon with such intensity that for an instant, she forgot where she was. She was fascinated by those eyes and what was behind them, she could lose herself in them if she wasn't careful, she could look at them forever, she could …

"Yes," Sharon said, "we can certainly do that." She brought up the revs of the engine, increasing the pitch of the rotors. The chopper lifted off, spun around and continued hugging the road. She brought a wad of Kleenex out her pocket.

"Here," she shouted, "you can use these."

As Breen reluctantly took the tissues, Sharon noticed he was leaning toward the open space where the door would have been.

"Why are you leaning out of the chopper like that? You could fall!" she shouted.

Breen didn't hear. He was busy studying traffic below through binoculars and fighting blind, unrelenting panic.

....

The mesa just north of the town of Quartzsite off Route 95 was a favorite place of hang gliding enthusiasts. A high, broad plateau rising above the valley with sharp, rocky slopes, it was ideally suited to the sport due to its strong updrafts. But it was the middle of the week and the members of the Falcon's Club all had day jobs … except for the lone glider who had just soared off White's Cliff and was circling back now, taking advantage of the updraft as it caught him and was pushing him higher than he'd been in years.

He'd just gotten his pink slip from McDonnell Douglas who'd announced that cutbacks were possible several months ago. He never thought it would happen to him, but he was a relatively new employee, having been there only five years.

His job as a word processor was not a high priority one and the cutbacks had affected one hundred fifty people, mostly those in similar positions. He was lucky. A single guy with no family, he knew he'd be okay. But many of the people had families, responsibilities. Some of them were in big trouble. But they weren't his concern now. He'd come here to get away from the pressures; he was being rewarded

with one of the most fantastic views in his hang-glid-
ing experience.

The day was exceptionally clear with not a
cloud in sight. As he soared high above the cliff, he
had a spectacular, sweeping view of the desert and
surrounding mountains. To the northeast he could see
the Montezuma Castle National Monument. Directly
east, I-17 snaked south toward Phoenix with the few
cars on it looking like tiny dark spots against the
earth; thirty miles to the south, Lake Pleasant was a
slash of blue and he could see the Gila River mean-
dering across the landscape like a piece of string
thrown carelessly on the ground. But the new element today was black smoke rising to the south, not
far from Quartzsite.

He caught an updraft and glided south into an
area he'd never seen before. On a plateau that
peaked in a high crest of rocks, he noticed an old dirt
road that zig-zagged up in a series of switchbacks
past a hogback and finally ended near the crest. Then
he saw the valley below, one he didn't know existed.

Stretching for miles between two surrounding
plateaus, it was a vast, barren patch of desert with
cacti and sagebrush broken up with an occasional
stand of mesquite. He soared over the valley … and
then he saw the source of the smoke.

It appeared to be some kind of building. What it was doing in this isolated area he had no idea. Why would anyone want a building out here with no means of access? As he neared the burning structure, he carefully steered around it knowing the turbulence rising from the fire could send him crashing to earth. He circled the site twice, noted his position, then caught an updraft and soared away past the smoking debris, forgetting the incident as he prepared to re-turn to earth and its nagging practicalities, including job hunting in the morning.

....

The police chopper was nearing the configuration of interconnecting highways where I-19 split off from I-10 and turned south. Sharon glanced at Breen. He was studying the traffic below, holding the binoculars in his left hand while leaning toward the opening on the side of the chopper as if he was about to jump. She squelched the impulse to ask him what the hell was going on and looked back down at the freeway.

"Should we go with I-19 or I-10?" she said as they approached the intersection.

"Stay with I-10," Breen said. He was perspiring so heavily now that it was dripping off his chin and soaking his pants legs. Suddenly he shouted into the headset, "Take it down, TAKE IT DOWN!"

"Do you see something?"

"No, just take it down!"

"Okay, okay," Sharon said looking quickly for a landing spot. Before she could find one, Breen overcame his wave of fear, wiped his forehead and leaned back.

"Forget it, I'm okay, take it up …"

Sharon glanced at Breen. "Which is it, up or down?"

"Up, up," he said, "keep going!"

"Whatever you say," Sharon said, hiding a smile, "I'm here to serve."

The chopper flared up as Breen went back to his vigil. "We should have caught up with them by now, what the hell happened?" He glanced out the window and noticed that the chopper was climbing. "You're getting too high, stay low, STAY LOW!!"

The urgency in Manny's voice was real but there was so much panic in it, it seemed exaggerated. Sharon couldn't help it. She smiled out loud.

"What am I, a yo-yo?"

Breen ignored her. He looked down and was studying a knot of trucks and cars following each other in a pack. *It was funny the way that happened,* he thought, *cars clumped together like caravans on the desert leaving vast spaces where there were no vehicles at all. Maybe they clung together for company.*

The Notar had just passed over a moving van with the letters "A Moving Experience" painted on the sides …then a van and a Honda … and now Manny saw the truck. It was big enough to be the right size. He swung the glasses past it to the road ahead. It was alone. He swept back to the truck.

"Take it lower," he said. This time the urgency in his voice was without fear.

Alerted, Sharon glanced down.

"It's big enough," Breen said. "But it has the wrong coloring. Also, the plates are different, it has the wrong lettering on the sides."

"Maybe they split up," Sharon said as they zoomed over the truck.

"Maybe, but they couldn't change their color," Manny said as he relaxed slightly, then remembered where he was, dropping the glasses to his knees. "Can you get closer to the ground?"

Sharon shook her head and smiled. "If I get any closer to the ground, we'll have to register with the DMV." She was certain now that she knew what was happening to Det. Breen. She looked at him. "You're claustrophobic, aren't you?"

"No, it's the flu," Manny said in a weak attempt to cover up his phobia.

"Look," Sharon said sympathetically, "a lot of people have phobias, it's not a crime. I have a friend who's got the same problem. Know how she beats it? She closes her eyes and takes a deep breath … then she takes the next breath … she says to herself, 'I've got plenty of oxygen, I can breathe, I'm okay … I'm okay.'"

Breen was a man. Men didn't admit to weakness of any kind, did they? Especially not to a woman.

"I'm not claustrophobic," he said, trying to convince himself, "but stay low to the ground, okay?" He looked at Sharon. Those eyes again. But this time they were pleading like a little kid who needed help.

....

The trucks had successfully changed appearances and split up to throw off the authorities. With new plates, different coloring and new company names, the only thing still unchanged was their mammoth size. As the lone sister truck approached the southernmost part of Tucson on I-19, it took the cut off to Valencia Road and headed due east passing the Tucson International Airport. A few moments later it arrived at I-10 where the second truck was waiting along with Fazio's convoy that had caught up with the truck a few moments before. Inside the Honda, Fazio smiled as the second truck fell in behind its sister.

Instead of continuing southeast, the trucks headed back northwest on I-10.

"Why are they going back?" J.J. said as the Honda followed the trucks.

"Two reasons," Fazio said. "One, no one expects us to reverse course. Two, Casa Grande is halfway between Luke and Davis Air Force Bases. We can hit both simultaneously within a short time-frame. The missiles won't be airborne long enough to be detected by radar."

J.J. Fryer smiled. "Oshiba's thought of every thing."

"Everything. I'm particularly interested in taking out Davis. That's where they train pilots on the A-10 Warthog."

"The plane that killed Vince, Jr."

Fazio nodded, then slowly, "The plane that killed Vince, Jr."

"J.J. glanced at his friend. What he saw was an iron mask of determination mixed with a virulent, seething hatred.

....

The trucks with convoy turned east on McCartney Road away from Casa Grande to a location less populated, then turned off on a deserted dirt road and stopped a quarter of a mile from the main road. Not far away, Picacho Peak and the Santa Catalina mountains were visible.

The trucks stood poised, engines throbbing, like two pulsing demons about to strike.

....

No one could have dreamed that the technology needed to build the trucks' sophisticated weapon systems could have been developed so quickly. But that was because they didn't know Billy Oshiba, one of the great geniuses in the microchip industry. Oshiba, with an IQ of one hundred eighty plus, had received his training in Japan where he'd worked for Fujitsu, Ltd. developing their VP2400/40 Super

Computer system and the software package that went with it. This had taken place in the late eighties. He'd gone independent and was close to a breakthrough on building the first Teraflop Super Computer System when Vincent Fazio, Sr. heard about him and brought him into the fold.

With Fazio's money, the work had gone forward at a blistering pace, allowing Oshiba to make his breakthrough in late 1991. When the dust settled, the brilliant young Asian had created a super computer that operated through massive parallel processing; the Teraflops could process trillions of bits of information simultaneously. Result: The super trucks were the deadliest weapons on earth.

They could outfight, outshoot, outthink, and outmaneuver any other weapon systems in the early nineties as well as those on the drawing board that would become operational in the next ten years. The trucks were the fulfillment of Alvin Toffler's prediction in his 1991 book, "Powershift," that speed was the God of the 21st century and that the degree of speed with which nations or entities could gather, calculate, assimilate, and disperse knowledge would determine their survival or destruction.

With a bank of Teraflop Super Computers in each truck linked by a built-in command center similar to that of the current AWACS Air Force planes, the computers' electronic jammers could send out an infinite array of high-energy pulses that would disorient hostile radar; they could sniff out an enemy's frequencies and then throw out false signals to fog his radar display; they carried an advanced phased-array radar system that allowed the trucks' radar to track multiple enemy targets. But the piece de resistance: Oshiba's own little invention.

He called it his MFD System, the initials standing for Multiple Fractionalized Displacement. It operated by projecting not just pulses but actual false images of the trucks which confused enemy sensors and spooked their radar screens so that they wouldn't know which target to hit.

Finishing off the MFD was Oshiba's High Energy Magnetic Field System that deflected enemy fire. Even if they figured out which image was the real one, they couldn't hit it anyway and by then it would be too late. The trucks' attack programs and hardware, even more sophisticated than their defense systems, would have already annihilated the enemy.

Twelve computers were lined up in the center aisle of each truck. A powerful air conditioner held the temperature at a cool fifty degrees keeping them from "sweating," and enabling the units to operate at full potential. Four Chinese Multiple Launch Rocket Systems with nineteen tubes each were mounted on either side just behind the cabs. This gave the trucks an unparalleled high-firing density. In less than ten seconds, they could blanket an area with one hundred fifty two missiles.

Adapted to use the American ATACMs, they had an increased range of over three hundred miles. The payloads varied from the conventional to sophisticated chemical/biological warheads, but the most destructive weapon the trucks carried was the more than dozen fuel-air-explosives, each with the clout of a small atomic bomb.

The delivery system for the fuel-air bombs was the AGM High-Speed Anti-Radiation Missile (HARM), a deadly missile with a speed of Mach 2, a missile so fast with smokeless motors that it could close the distance to the target before anyone realized it had been fired.

Six superheated gas cannons that could propel shells twice as fast as an ordinary cannon were placed strategically around each truck's perimeter. Various booby traps would dissuade any intruder from trying to gain entrance to the interiors of these engineering marvels.

The small compact engines were so cool that they virtually had no acoustic or infrared signature. This meant that infrared sights on attacking planes that could detect a target barely over half of one degree Celsius warmer than its surroundings couldn't find it. Machine guns were installed in the front, rear and both sides of both trucks which were activated when a hostile actor was near.

Completing the package was ceramic armor plating made with special composite materials and non-radioactive uranium separated by air spaces.

Combined with a rounded design, this amalgamation of elements would deflect even a tungsten rod fired from an M1 tank.

If the trucks had one flaw, it was the need to refuel every three hundred eighty miles. Most eighteen wheelers had the capacity to carry eight hundred gallons of diesel fuel stored in two four hundred gallon tanks, one on either side of each vehicle. Due to the heavy load of military ordinance in each truck, Oshiba had been forced to settle for two one hundred gallon tanks for each behemoth, giving them slightly over two miles per gallon. The necessity for frequent refueling had created a need to secure a number of gas stations stretching east along the I-10 corridor, a task the Asian had masterminded with pinpoint accuracy.

....

Inside the Honda, Fazio and J.J. glanced simultaneously at their watches.

The trucks, engines idling, had pulled off the road onto the desert floor.

"There it is," Fazio said. "Zero ten hundred hours coming up. The first missiles should fire in … twenty seconds."

Inside the trucks, the computers engaged in a sudden flurry of activity, spitting out data and running numbers at a blinding rate of speed. The electronic radar jammers were activated. As a digital clock ticked down to fifteen seconds, the activity increased as panels on the left side of the rear truck slid up. The blunt, ugly tubes of the MLRS thrust forward mechanically, slowly increasing its vertical pitch to a firing position.

As the clock reached zero, two missiles carrying FAE warheads exploded out of the tubes, arched high, and disappeared over the horizon, leaving a fiery trail.

Fazio pushed a button located under the seat of the Honda. The dashboard slid back revealing a TV screen which went from black to a sudden view from the nose of the lead missile.

....

Luke Air Force Base was located in Maricopa County in a flat stretch of desert just west of I-10 between Phoenix and Tucson. Along with Davis Monthan just south of Tucson, the two bases constituted a military complex devoted in large part to the testing and development of new weapon systems as well as being a training ground for new pilots. The vast, empty spaces of the southwest made it an ideal location for this testing and training while offering a low probability of civilian casualties if anything went wrong.

The Jeep carrying Commander Larry Torchio screeched to a stop in front of Central Command Headquarters. In charge of the Aerial Combat Maneuvers Adversary Training Unit attached to the US Army's 160th Special Operations Aviation Regiment, the Bronx born fighter "jock" was perfect for his job.

Torch, as his wingmen called him, had logged over 5,000 hours beginning with the F-4 in Viet Nam and graduating to the F-16, F-111 and the classy F-117A Stealth fighter in the Gulf War.

Today he'd planned to lead a special four-plane mission to 'defend' the Javeline Mountain located at the eastern fringes of the gunnery range from 'enemy' attack, but he'd aborted the mission the day before. Due to sloppy 'shooting' on the previous days' exercises, Torch had decided to take a day off and work with his team on aerial gunnery against a towed target.

Setting up the aerial gunnery exercise on such short notice hadn't been easy. First he'd contacted Edwards Air Force Base in California. They'd agreed to loan him a TDU-10B 'dart' target and its concomitant towing system. The dart served his purposes perfectly. Only a quarter the size of most towed targets, it would severely challenge his pilots' accuracy.

His second call had gone out to the 148th FIG based at Duluth Municipal Airport. Torch needed a top-flight WSO.

The Weapon Systems Officer's job was to sit in the back seat of the aircraft and deploy the target at the exact instant. Improperly released, the target could separate from the cable holding it and cause the mission to be aborted. The 148th had sent one of its best WSO officers, Air Force Colonel Paul Mac-Intire, who'd been flown out the previous night in an air force F-111.

Before he got out of the Jeep, Commander Torchio, his mind spilling over a thousand details that had to be attended to before the exercise could get underway, looked casually up at the clear blue sky. As his orderly opened the door, he was still looking up thinking that it was a perfect day for flying when

he saw a missile appear overhead, then break up re-
leasing three canisters that began falling toward the
ground as parachutes billowed out above each one.

"What the hell …?"

....

Luke Air Force Base Command Post Radar Division
10:10 a.m. Mountain Time

A radar technician, looking at the screen, suddenly saw a blip approaching, and just as the blip appeared, the screen blurred and filled with lines.

"What the hell …?"

....

Jeep In Front of Command Post
10:10 a.m. Mountain Time

As Commander Torchio watched, something inside told him what was happening but he couldn't grasp it. The bomblets were getting closer now and when they reached thirty feet, they began dispersing aerosol fuel which formed a fine mist covering a large portion of the base. A few seconds later when the bomblets were almost upon them, a fuse in one of the canisters ignited the fuel vapor.

Commander Torchio's last impression was of an overpowering smell of gasoline as he was obliterated by the blast which was equal to the power of the atomic bomb that hit Hiroshima. The fuel-air explosion was followed by an intense pressure wave that destroyed all surface structures and aircraft at the Air Force Base. What occurred next was as lethal as the initial blast; a firestorm sucked the oxygen from the lungs of all personnel on the ground who were still alive.

The same scenario unfolded simultaneously over Davis Monthan Air Force Base, annihilating a crew working on a Longbow Apache on the runway, all parked aircraft, and everything else visible.

....

Deserted Dirt Road Near Luke and Davis Air Force
Bases
10:10 a.m. Mountain Time

Fazio and John Jamington Fryer watched on the
Honda's TV screen through cameras mounted in the
nose cones of the bomblets. Fazio flicked off the TV
monitor located on the front panel of the Honda.

"Like clockwork, Vince," J.J. said.

"Yes," Vincent Fazio said with a smile, "And
it's just the beginning!"

....

Airspace Over Tucson
10:10 a.m. Mountain Time

Manny and Sharon had just heard the two explosions thirty miles to the west. "Must have been thunder," Sharon said, as she maneuvered the chopper over the highway.

Manny was studying vehicles on the road below. "Yeah, or a new weapon at the air force base … something's wrong, we couldn't have missed 'em …"

Engulfed in a sudden wave of panic, Manny dropped the binoculars, closed his eyes, began breathing hard and struggling for control.

"What does she say? Your friend?"

"I can breathe, I'm okay …" Sharon said.

" … I can breathe … I'm okay …"

"Say it again."

"I can breathe, I'm okay …" Manny repeated.

Sharon studied him a moment, then … "Feel better?"

Manny opened his eyes and continued breathing deeply. "Yeah, I … think so, I …"

Beginning to lose it, his eyes widened. "I've got plenty of oxygen, I'm okay, I'm … Take it down, TAKE IT DOWN!"

"Okay, okay!" Sharon said, nodding, as she maneuvered the Notar toward the ground, "I'll stay low, we can touch down any time, okay?"

"Yeah, yeah, okay, okay. Okay," Manny said, calming down, "stay low."

They were silent a moment, then Manny looked at Sharon. "What's your name?"

"Sharon Kramer."

Suddenly Dispatch cut in. "Dispatch to 117CR. Where are you?"

Sharon checked her surroundings. "Thirty miles east of Tucson …"

The chopper turned. "… Now heading east again."

"Sharon," Michelle at Dispatch said, "somebody wants to talk to Manny Breen."

"Roger," Sharon said as she handed the mic to Manny.

"Breen," Manny said into the mic.

"Manny, it's Joey. We can't believe it, man! What the hell happened?"

Manny was close to breaking down. "I'll tell you later …"

"Look," Joey continued, "We got an APB out and we scrambled another chopper, we'll find those trucks, I guarantee it!"

Another voice came over the mic. "Breen, this is Chief Hunt. I know how you feel, I want you to come in ..."

Manny exploded. "You *don't* know how I fucking feel!"

Sharon's eyes were fastened on Manny.

"Look," Chief Hunt continued, "you're in no condition to deal with this now. You find those trucks you'll blow the drivers away, that's what I'd do if they killed my sister .. and I can't allow that." (Beat) "Breen?"

Manny handed the mic back to Sharon who was still staring at him.

"Breen?" Chief Hunt continued, "Officer Kramer? You turn that bird around and get back here right now or your ass is mud!"

A beat, Sharon made a quick decision. She tapped the transmission hook. "Experiencing transmission problems ...hello ... hello ..." She placed the radio mic back on the hook.

Manny was staring straight ahead. "Thanks."

"I can't tell you how sorry I am .."

Manny had been toughing it out, but the sympathy tore into him. His eyes filled with tears. "Just help me find the trucks."

....

Luke Air Force Base
10:25 a.m. Mountain Time

The initial blast and shock wave from the thermobaric explosion had caused horrific destruction. Structures were leveled, dead military personnel were everywhere, smoking hulls of voluminous aircraft littered the runways.

A Jeep sped up to the smoking ruins where the Command Post had been and screeched to a stop. An Air Force Major stood up in the Jeep and looked around.

"Holy Christ!" he muttered as the totality of the destruction dawned on him. Other Jeeps arrived and slammed on their brakes. Soldiers, guns drawn, jumped out and began exploring the wreckage.

....

The same scenario was unfolding at Davis. Planes were burning on the runways or blown to pieces as personnel began arriving in Jeeps.

....

The police chopper with Sharon and Manny was skimming the highway low over I-10 east.

Inside the Notar, the atmosphere was heavy. The two rode a moment without talking. Sharon was the first to break the silence.

"You're right about what you told the Chief. Nobody ever knows how another person feels. Grief is a very personal thing …"

Manny, intently studying the road below, said nothing.

. . . .

Service Station Near Bowie, Arizona
11:10 a.m. Mountain Time

Several cars and a few trucks were refueling as a black van sped up and skidded to an abrupt stop. A dozen men wearing masks jumped out carrying automatic weapons; several had hand-held missile-launchers. They dispersed like a military unit; some entered the station and shot all present; others killed all customers who were refueling.

Fazio's Honda approached and stopped. As Fazio and J.J. got out, a trucker who'd gone unnoticed by Fazio's men snuck into his truck, gunned the engine, and made a run for the entrance to I-10. One of Fazio's men saw the trucker heading for the exit, ran to the center of the station to get a clear shot, then fired a missile at the fleeing diesel. The projectile slammed into the truck obliterating it as Fazio ran to the shooter.

"You idiot! I told you, only use the MANPAD as a last resort! Now the whole fucking world will see the smoke!"

....

Route I-10 Off-Ramp Near The Captured Station
11:11 a.m. Mountain Time

Several of Fazio's men, dressed as construction workers, had the exit blocked off. A state trooper's car pulled up with the window rolled down.

"What's going on?" the trooper asked.

"Car caught on fire" one of the 'workers' said, "fire truck's on the way, everything's under control."

The trooper nodded, maneuvered around the barricade, and sped toward the station on the off ramp.

The 'worker' pulled out a walkie-talkie. "State police car coming in," he said into the mic.

. . . .

Service Station Near Bowie, Arizona
11:11 a.m. Mountain Time

Fazio was standing in the center of the station watching the incoming patrol car. "Roger," he replied into the walkie talkie. He whistled, motioning to his men around the station to take evasive action.

As the trooper approached the station, he slowed, warily observing the scene. A Chevrolet with the engine running was parked in front of a pump with the nozzle loose on the ground, a dead motorist hanging over the wheel; the window in the office was shattered, and more bodies could be seen in front of the office.

The trooper realized he was in danger, veered away, floored the accelerator and cut across the desert toward the highway as J.J. fired a burst at the fleeing officer from his automatic weapon hitting the trooper's car repeatedly, including the trooper, who slumped forward on the dashboard. The car slowed and stopped, horn blaring.

....

Route I-10 Off-Ramp Leading To The Captured Station
11:11 a.m. Mountain Time

The two super trucks had arrived, slowing as they approached the off-ramp. Fazio's men waved the trucks in, then replaced the barriers. The trucks moved along the off-ramp, then pulled into the station. As Fazio's men stood guard, Fazio approached the rear section of the lead truck, took out a gold key and inserted it into a side panel. The opened panel revealed a computer screen with a blinking red light. Fazio punched in a series of numbers, then smiled as he added a final seven digit code.

"Oshiba, you've got a weird sense of humor," he said to himself.

Inside the body of the lead truck, the words

ACCESS VERIFIED

appeared on a computer screen, while outside the truck, the refueling process had begun.

....

"You read a lot?" Manny said. He'd noticed half a dozen paperback books on the floor by Sharon's seat.

"Yes," Sharon replied, "it keeps my mind off chocolate. You were very close to your sister, weren't you?"

Manny nodded. "I brought her up." He raised the binoculars and studied the highway below. "Have any brothers or sisters?"

"Yes," Sharon said as she checked the fuel gauge. "My youngest brother, Buddy, was in the reserves. We were both in Desert Storm. I made it, he didn't."

Manny looked over as Sharon continued.

"Remember that one-in-a-million shot where the incoming Scud broke up? Our Tomahawk didn't know what to track?"

"You mean Khobar City? The barracks that took that direct hit?"

"Yes. We thought Bud was safe for sure, away from the front lines …"

"My God, Sharon, it's my turn to be sorry …"

A sudden panic swept over Manny; Sharon noticed.

"Stick your head out."

"Yeah, head." Manny leaned out and thrust his head into the fresh air as the chopper veered away.

. . . .

Davis Monthan Air Force Base
11:20 Mountain Time

A Jeep carrying Brig. General Alvin Hastings had just arrived on the base. The scene was one of total destruction: the buildings were smoking shells, bodies were strewn across the runways, and burning planes were being extinguished by first responders.

Hastings exited the Jeep and approached a Lt. Colonel who'd been inspecting a damaged Wart Hog. "What happened here, Colonel?"

"Looks like we got hit by some kind of bomb, sir."

The General nodded. "Same damn thing happened at Luke. I want a full report on my desk by 0-1200 hours. We're setting up a tent near the old command center. What's that odor?"

"Smells like high octane fuel."

"I want this kept quiet until we know what we're dealing with here."

"Yes, sir."

Hastings stepped back in his Jeep and sped away, tires screeching, through dense smoke and burning buildings.

....

Service Station Near Bowie, Arizona
11:35 a.m. Mountain Time

The two super trucks, fully refueled, pulled out of the station. The van followed onto the access road to I-10 East.

Before leaving the station, Fazio and J.J. made a final check. Fazio saw a motorist stirring beside his car, walked over and put a bullet through the man's head. A second motorist saw the murder and played dead as the two men, convinced there were no survivors, entered the Honda and followed the trucks.

....

The chopper was flying low to the ground. Traffic below was light, mostly with cars and a few trucks.

Inside the chopper, Sharon had opened a bag of nuts. She offered some to Manny. He declined, intent on the traffic below.

Manny's frustration was growing as he mentally qualified each large vehicle on the freeway, eliminating each one.

"You flew a chopper in the Gulf War?"

"Chinook, bringing in ammo," Sharon said, checking the sky above them. "I was one of twenty-two female pilots."

"101st Airborn?"

"Right. Wanted to fly an Apache, they wouldn't let me."

"That explains why you're so good."

"I've been flying since I was ten. My dad owns Mesa Charter Service."

As Manny was studying the road below, Sharon tapped him on the shoulder and pointed toward the horizon.

"Look."

Manny looked in the direction Sharon was pointing and saw a voluminous column of smoke rising, approximately twenty miles ahead.

"We'd better take a look."

"Roger," Sharon said, nosing the aircraft south, southeast.

....

Service Station Off I-10 at Bowie, AZ
11:50 a.m. Mountain Time

A few minutes later, the Notar arrived over the smoking truck and the trooper's car in the sand.

"What happened here?" Sharon said.

"Set it down over by that trooper's car."

"Roger."

Sharon's chopper circled the station, then touched down in the sand in front of the pumps. Manny jumped out and ran to the trooper's bullet-riddled car with the horn still blaring. He knew the officer was dead but checked his pulse to be sure. Next, he ran to the truck and found another dead civilian.

After checking the other casualties inside the office and the perimeter around the station, Manny was returning to the chopper when he heard a moan coming from a car near one of the gas pumps. He ran to the car, found a wounded motorist slumped against the wheel, pulled the man from the car and laid him on the ground as Sharon ran over and began performing CPR.

"What happened?"

The man coughed and spoke in a whisper. "Guys wearing masks … jumped out of a van … started shooting … they just … started shooting …"

"Was it a robbery?"

"No, they …" The man paused, coughed again and spit blood … "they refueled two big trucks … why did they kill all these people … just to …"

Manny and Sharon exchanged looks. "Can you describe the trucks?"

The man shook his head. "Huge … they were … huge trucks … rust colored, Jersey plates …"

Manny looked startled. "Jersey plates? You sure?"

The man nodded. "Yeah … one guy wasn't … wasn't wearing a mask … he murdered one of the wounded people, just came over and shot him in the head …"

"Can you describe him?" The man nodded.

"Big guy, lot of hair …"

An Arizona State Police car skidded to a halt near Manny. A trooper jumped out, gun drawn, and approached. "What the hell's going on here?"

"Put out an APB on two trucks, big diesels, rust bodies with black domes, New Jersey plates heading for New Mexico. And call for an ambulance!"

"Who are you?"

Manny and Sharon started for the chopper as Manny flashed his badge.

"Get a sketch artist out here. That motorist can describe one of the perps …"

As they climbed inside, Sharon looked at Manny. "Our trucks?"

"I don't know, the description's different, but we should be able to catch up with them on thirty-five."

"Think it's a terrorist operation?"

"Or drugs. They run 'em up from Mexico all the time."

"But why hit a service station and massacre everybody just to refuel two trucks?"

"Maybe their credit card expired," Manny said as the radio crackled. "117CR, this is … bombs at … and Marana …" The transmission kept breaking up.

"Dispatch? We can't hear you, must be an electrical storm brewing. Try us later," Sharon said into the mic.

. . . .

TV Station KPHO In Phoenix
12:15 p.m. Mountain Time

Since news of the two huge blasts at Luke and Davis
Monthan Air Force Bases earlier in the morning, TV
stations had been fighting to be the first ones to
break the story of who, what, why and when. KPHO
was no exception. There was frantic activity in the
newsroom as an on-camera announcer was speaking
with great urgency.

"… and at this point in time, nobody knows
what caused the two explosions, but there has been
speculation that terrorism cannot be ruled out.
There's no cause for alarm, I repeat …"

In the control booth, an associate producer with
breaking news hurried over to the producer who was
standing at the back of the room with a bevy of TV
personnel.

"It was some kind of bomb, hit both Davis and
Luke … at least two thousand, five hundred dead,
nearly total destruction of aircraft on both fields …!"

"Jesus!" the producer said, "What the hell's going on?" He addressed the AP with great urgency.
"Get a unit out to Luke, it's closer!"

The associate producer nodded. "I've already
done that …"

The producer turned to his secretary who was
waiting with pen and notepad at the ready. "Get the

sheriff on the phone and Commander Beal at the National Guard in Tucson …"

"Yes, sir!" the secretary said as she hurried back to her desk.

Before the AP could leave the control booth, the producer called to him. "Jerry? Any indication of what type bomb?"

"Not yet," the AP said …

"Okay, go! Go!" Then, to another AP standing at his side, "Cancel all programming and get in touch with the Pentagon. We have to find out what the hell's going on …"

"Yes, sir!" The AP said, heading back to his computer.

………

Up until the present, Breen had been so focused on finding the trucks that his claustrophobia had not surfaced. Now, it was sneaking back into his mind like a predatory weasel.

Images of the accident flooded in: Betsy's car flying through the air, the burning hulk, the searing heat from the flames as he tried to reach her, the brilliant flash from the truck. With a supreme effort, he blotted out the image and tried to focus on what Sharon had told him her friend had said. "I can breathe, I'm okay,"… but it wasn't working.

Sharon was acutely aware of Manny's turmoil. She was working with a problem of her own. All her life she'd over-sympathized with people, felt what they were feeling, tried to help. This tendency had gotten her a lot of pain; others had taken advantage of her good heart.

She squelched an impulse to touch Manny's hand. Finally, she reached a compromise with her feelings and settled for the practical. "Want me to take it down?"

Manny shook his head. "No, it's okay … I can breathe … I can … I'm okay."

As Manny and Sharon were fighting their personal demons in the chopper, they were skimming

low over a moving van with the words "A Moving
Experience" painted on the sides.

……….

Port of Entry Inspection Station At Arizona/New
Mexico Border
12:21 p.m. Mountain Time

An agent inside the office near the entry lanes had just answered the phone.

"Hello, this is Willie ..." He listened, then nodded. "Yeah, two of 'em?" Another pause, then ... "Okay, we'll be ready."

....

I-10 East Several Miles West of the Station
12:22 p.m. Mountain Time

The two super trucks, speeding down I-10, zipped by a state patrol car hiding near a grove of apple trees. The trooper hit his siren and took off in pursuit, approaching the rear truck at high speed.

The truck slowed. At its back end, a panel slid up, a nozzle sprang forward and began spewing a stream of liquid fire. It struck the trooper's car enveloping it in flames. The trooper screamed as his car spun out of control, soared over the embankment, and exploded.

A motorist traveling behind the patrol car slowed and stopped. The driver jumped out and tried to reach the flaming mass, but the heat was too great.

The Notar approached, circled above the scene, then settled down on the shoulder as Manny hopped out and ran to the motorist standing at the door of his car.

"What happened?"

The motorist was in shock. "The patrol car was chasing a huge diesel … and suddenly this flame shot out …"

"From the truck?"

"Yes …"

Manny looked at the burning wreck and saw there was no way he could save the trooper. "Rust colored? Jersey plates?"

"I think so …"

"I'll call it in, stay here and tell the authorities what you saw!"

Manny ran back to the chopper idling on the shoulder and hopped in. "The trooper's car was stopped by a flame thrower mounted in one of the trucks."

Sharon glanced over at the burning vehicle. "I'm beginning to wish I was flying an Apache."

………

Davis Mothan Air Force Base
12:30 p.m. Mountain Time

Fires were still raging in what was left of buildings on the base. Fragments of destroyed aircraft littered the runways as firemen worked to put out the conflagration and fire engines kept arriving from Scottsdale, Mesa, Peoria, Buckeye, Surprise, and Apache Junction to assist in the cleanup.

A contingent from the National Guard had been deployed, as well as various police personnel from the surrounding area. A number of EMS crews were attending the wounded, as well as first responders from the Mayo Clinic-Phoenix, Banner Estrella Medical Center, St. Joseph's Hospital, Banner Boswell Medical Center, Chandler Regional Medical Center and many others.

A makeshift operations center had been set up in a tent where the Command Center stood before the blast. A TV truck was parked nearby with a unit filming the devastation as a second unit filmed a reporter from KPHO addressing the camera.

" … and Brigadier General Hastings just entered the tent which is serving as the makeshift base …We'll keep you up to date as we receive information as to the cause of the attack, how it was accomplished, and who was responsible."

Inside the tent, General Hastings was seated in a folding chair in front of a card table as the Lt. Colonel hurried in and saluted. "What have you got, Colonel?"

"Sir, according to reports coming in from both bases, a lot of the dead died of suffocation."

Hastings looked startled. "What?"

"Yes, sir," the Colonel replied, "several survivors described a heavy smell of fuel before the blast, then a firestorm. Suddenly they couldn't breathe."

"Colonel," Hastings said, his face sombre, "you just described a fuel-air explosion."

The Colonel nodded. "Yes, sir."

"An FAE has to be detonated in the air. That means it was either dropped from a plane or a chopper or delivered by a missile. Any reports of aircraft in the area before the blasts?"

"No, sir, I checked it out."

Hastings, deep in thought, drummed his fingers on the table. "Then it had to come from a missile. How the hell's that possible with all our sophisticated detection equipment?"

"A radar man who survived said they experienced interference just before the bomb hit. It blacked out their screens."

"They jammed us? *THEY JAMMED US?!* What the hell … !

………..

The chopper had just flown over an underpass. Manny, who'd been scrutinizing it in his binoculars, had an intuition.

"Circle back, let's check that underpass."

"Roger."

The Notar curved around, approached the location and dropped down in front of the entrance, hovering just above the ground. Manny reached back and grabbed a rifle from the gun rack. "Wait for me at the other end."

"I'm coming with you!"

"Uh, uh, keep trying to get through."

Manny hopped out, ran toward the underpass, and entered it as the chopper lifted off.

. . . .

The Underpass On Route I-10
1:11 p.m. Mountain Time

Barely visible in the dark, the two trucks were stopped, engines idling. At the back end of the rear truck, a machine-gun barrel appeared above the tailpipe as Manny entered the underpass. Sensing danger, Breen dove to the ground firing as the machine gun bursts hit the space where he'd been standing.

The trucks' lights flipped on as the two monsters headed for daylight.

Manny's rifle rounds bounced off the body of the trucks causing small explosions.

At the far end of the underpass, the police chopper was hovering near the exit, and as the trucks burst into daylight, Sharon instinctively maneuvered the chopper up and away.

Inside the rear truck, a computer screen lit up showing a blip on the screen with the blinking words, "Enemy Aircraft 100 Meters." The chopper blip was immediately illuminated and held in the center of the kill zone.

Outside the truck, the MLRS panel slid up as Manny ran out of the underpass in time to see the rear truck fire a missile at the chopper.

"Holy shit!"

Sharon had moved the aircraft behind a bridge support just in time, causing the missile to slam into the abutment, destroying it and causing minor damage to the chopper. The helicopter touched down in a nearby field as a second police chopper zoomed in from nowhere flying low over the tunnel, closing fast on the huge vehicles.

Manny yelled, "GET BACK! THEY HAVE MISSILES! DON'T —" as another missile ripped into the second police chopper, blowing it to bits. Manny, on the run toward the Notar, was beginning to realize what he was up against. "Son-of-a-bitch! SON-OF-A-BITCH!" he yelled.

. . . .

Standing on a hill overlooking I-10, Fazio and J.J. were observing the battle through binoculars.

"We don't have to worry about the trucks, they can take care of themselves!" Fazio said, lowering the binoculars.

J.J. nodded, then glanced at his watch. "We're right on time!" They entered the Honda and drove off.

. . . .

Manny saw Sharon exit the chopper and run toward the burning aircraft. He caught up and tackled her. "What the hell do you think you're doing?"

"That was one of ours! I knew the pilot …!"

"There's nothing you can do for them … come on."

When Manny glanced at Sharon, tears were streaming down her face.

They both looked at the downed chopper as secondary explosions demolished what was left of the aircraft. Manny protected Sharon with his body.

"Come on, we've got to alert the army, the FBI …"

"We can't," Sharon said, "the radio's dead."

"Can we fly?"

"I don't know …"

They ran to the Notar; Sharon did a quick inspection. "A chunk of concrete hit the tail section, but we should be okay."

"Let's go!" Manny yelled.

Sharon started the engine, the blades rotated, the chopper lifted off. "Did you do any damage?"

Manny laughed. "You kidding? They're protected by ceramic block armor!"

As they skimmed low over I-10 going east, Sharon's face was drawn. She was silent, her mind racing. "I'll tell you one thing," she finally said, measuring her words carefully, "these guys aren't terrorists."

Manny studied her. "How do you know?"

"Terrorists are independent. They're usually a group of individuals who act on their own, like Abu Nadal or Black September." She paused. "It took a lot of time and manpower to engineer this, to coordinate the commando raid on the gas station. It's more like a military operation."

"How do you know so much about terrorism?"

Sharon shrugged. "I read everything."

. . . .

I-10 was comparatively empty as the trucks resumed their mission and sped east going over a hundred mph.

. . . .

Port of Entry Inspection Station, The Arizona/New Mexico Border
1:28 p.m. Mountain Time

The station was bristling with State Police cars and personnel. Troopers were standing behind their cars with guns ready. Barriers and road blocks were being constructed as the Police Captain marshaled his forces.

"Listen up, boys! We got a couple of renegade trucks headin' this way. They're not gonna stop, so let's give 'em a sweet surprise! Lock And Load!"

....

The first to see the trucks was a trooper who was standing on top of his squad car. "HERE THEY COME!" he shouted as he jumped down.

The trucks had appeared a quarter of a mile away zooming over a slight rise in the interstate. They were approaching the station at over a hundred mph, but then did the unexpected … they began to slow. By the time they were within fifty yards of the station, they were going under ten mph.

The Police Captain was puzzled by the trucks' maneuver. Caught off guard, he was staring at the beasts, not sure what to do as they came to a full stop ten yards from the station.

There was a long pause … then a loudspeaker on one of the trucks began blasting out a recording of Mr. Rogers singing, "It's A Wonderful Day In The Neighborhood". The policemen and troopers had varying reactions from confusion to astonishment.

The Captain motioned his men to move forward cautiously, guns leveled.

A trooper approached the cab of the first truck, and while others held their guns on the cab door, he reached for the door handle.

The same approach was made to the second truck by other troopers and police personnel. The instant the first trooper placed his hand on the door handle, a powerful electric current shot through him and knocked him ten feet off the ground. He landed twenty feet away and lay dead on the pavement, his body smoking.

The same scenario took place as a trooper tried to enter the second truck.

An official looking under the body of the lead truck was nailed with a puff of poisonous gas as another official, trying to enter at the rear of the truck, was also gassed.

Without warning, the windows of both trucks' cabs rolled down. A grayish yellow mist shot out over the heads of the remaining authorities, killing them instantly.

After all the bodies were still, the only remaining sound was Mr. Rogers' gentle voice singing, "It's a Wonderful Day In The Neighborhood ..."

The windows on both trucks closed as they adroitly navigated around the accumulated State Police cars and numerous bodies, then casually continued east on I-10.

....

The aircraft was skimming the freeway several miles west of the Inspection Station, paralleling the highway. Breen was glued to the road below. Traffic was lined up for miles. Horns were honking, motorists were getting out of their cars, straining to see what was holding up traffic.

"There's another problem up ahead," Manny said, pointing.

"Yeah, I see the jam-up," Sharon replied.

"What's the fuel situation?"

She looked down at the fuel gage. "We have a capacity of around four hundred seventy miles. We've traveled two hundred miles, I may have to find a place to refuel."

They rode in silence a moment. "These guys really know what they're doing," Sharon said. "Modern warfare is built on three factors: speed, precision, and surprise. They've utilized all three. The question is, what's their objective? And where were they constructed? You'd need access to modern technology, scads of money, a secret facility, maybe someplace in the northwest ..."

The chopper was approaching the Inspection Station. Manny followed the line of stalled cars, raised the binoculars, and looked a mile ahead down the road to the Station. What he saw made him swear.

"What's the matter, what do you see?"

Breen was focused on the Inspection Station and didn't hear.

"What the hell!" He was beginning to see more and more bodies littering the scene at the Station. He swept the binoculars to the right of the Station and picked up a hawk flying toward it several hundred feet in the air.

As it neared the Station, it suddenly faltered, then plummeted from the sky.

Manny quickly swept the binoculars back to the Station, judged the distance, then moved back once again to the hawk, now flopping helplessly on the ground.

"TAKE IT UP, QUICK!" he yelled.

The chopper veered left and lifted sharply in a vertical climb. "Go around and come in from up wind!"

"What is it?"

"Some kind of chemical agent."

"Oh, my God!"

The Notar circled around and approached from a different direction. It hovered low over the ground several hundred yards from the Station as Manny studied the carnage through his binoculars.

"Are you sure?"

Manny nodded. "A hawk downwind just got a taste of it … take it higher."

The chopper shot up quickly a hundred feet as Manny swept I-10 further east.

"THERE THEY ARE!" he said, pointing.

Sharon saw the trucks and opened the throttle.

"Don't get too close …"

"Right," Sharon said as the aircraft moved a half mile south and stayed a short distance behind the two monsters.

As Breen observed the two killers, he suddenly realized how they were able to evade detection. They began to transform, changing color and license plates.

"So that's how they do it," he said, handing the binoculars to Sharon. She trained them on the trucks as they completed their transformation.

"They've thought of everything," she said as the Notar shuddered and began to drop.

"Oh, oh," Sharon said, checking the instrument panel.

"Are we going to crash?" Manny said, grabbing the sides of his seat.

"Not if I can help it!" Sharon shouted.

The chopper dropped down erratically, then landed safely in the desert near I-10.

Manny pulled the rifle from the gun rack, grabbed some extra rounds, and threw the binoculars around his neck. He headed for a roadside diner on the other side of I-10.

"C'mon! Let's check out that diner!"

He and Sharon ran across I-10 into the diner's parking lot. "Notify the FBI and the local authorities about the poison gas at the Inspection Station, and call Joey Payne, Homicide Division. Ask Joey to check with D.C. about ceramic block contractors. I'll stay with the trucks!"

"How can you …?"

Manny ran to a Harley-Davidson parked in front of the diner. He shouted over his shoulder, "I was a motorcycle cop before I made detective!" He quickly hot-wired the cycle, hopped on, gunned the engine, and took off as the irate owner ran out of the diner waving his arms and yelling.

As Manny sped away, Sharon took the owner's name and address, explained that he'd get his vehicle back, that this was necessary for national security, then went inside and made two calls.

....

I-10 East in New Mexico
1:45 p.m. Mountain Time

After leveling the Inspection Station at the Arizona/ New Mexico border, the trucks had reached another target-rich area.

The Land of Enchantment was home to four Air Force Bases: Cannon AFB in Curry, Holloman in Otero, Kirkland in Bernalilio, and one of the great prizes in Fazio's sights, White Sands Missile Range, the largest AFB in the United States.

White Sands was so huge it was spread over five counties. Oshiba had had a field day constructing and planning this attack: one FAE each for the first three bases, and three for White Sands due to its size.

After traveling ten miles into New Mexico, the trucks took an exit, turned off on a deserted side road and stopped, engines idling, out of sight of I-10. The convoy was close behind.

The flat, barren landscape of sand peppered with cacti that engulfed the trucks, a scene of primitive monotony, was about to be shattered by a flurry of dramatic action. But for a tense moment, the desert was quiet. All that could be heard was the screech of a red-tailed hawk circling overhead and the sound of a lizard scuttling down a rock formation. A brief shower an hour earlier had perfumed the air with the sweet smell of wet sage and creosote.

Suddenly a beat-up pickup truck appeared, driving toward the trucks on the dirt road. The vehicle maneuvered around the super trucks and stopped across from the Honda. An elderly farmer in the vehicle wearing a cowboy hat and overalls waved through the open window.

"Hey? What're these trucks doin' here?" the old guy said with a smile.

Fazio rolled down the window of the Honda and shot the man between the eyes. The farmer fell forward over the wheel, blood already dripping on the seat.

"Wrong place, wrong time," Vincent said as the panels on the trucks slid up, the weapon systems were activated, the missiles were fired.

"Another gift for the Air Force," Fazio said to J.J., who nodded.

"Another gift for the Air Force," J.J. repeated with a wry smile as the trucks turned around in the desert after disgorging their venom and headed back to I-10 East. Fazio and the convoy followed as the behemoths led the way.

....

Breen had adjusted quickly to driving a two-wheeler again. He zoomed across the strip of desert between the diner and the highway, whipped onto I-10 East, revved the engine, and within a few seconds was speeding down the highway at over one hundred mph. He found a pair of goggles attached to the bike handle and slipped them on. Next, he checked the chamber of the rifle and slipped in another clip.

And Manny was in luck. The motorcycle's owner had just filled the tank.

Breen, unaware of the new attacks, felt more confident about finding the trucks. He knew more about them. It had been a quick learning process, from the belief that they were two ordinary trucks with drivers to the comprehension that these babies were something extra special. He'd had verification from talking to a victim of the attack at the gas station and now he'd witnessed the truck's ability to transform. They were diabolically devised weapons of mass annihilation constructed for a single purpose: kill and wreak destruction.

Manny wove expertly between cars and trucks on the flat, one-way stretch of two-lane highway as it meandered through the Chihuahuan Desert that seemed to stretch on endlessly. The dry arid land of the rugged Rocky Mountains, desert grasslands, azure skies, mesa tops, and spectacular canyons occupied most of New Mexico, Mexico and Texas. The speed limit here was eighty, but traffic was moving a lot faster, the average speed being around ninety-five.

Manny knew thet rucks would be speeding, but he was also aware that they had a mission. Just what, he didn't know, but part of that mission must be to remain anonymous, not to be noticed, even with their enormous size. He was confident he could catch the beasts because of the Harley's ability to move in and out of traffic at a higher rate of speed than the trucks would be traveling.

Breen realized the weather was cooling. In Phoenix, he'd always worn a sweater tied around his waist even on hot days due to his schedule. When he was working on a case, sometimes for three or four days without stop, the desert was often cold at night, even in summer. He'd learned to keep extra clothing in the car and the sweater came in handy. Now, in New Mexico, more than a hundred miles from home base, I-10 had been climbing steadily.

After passing Lordsburg, Manny was approaching the Great Atlantic/Pacific Continental Divide where the elevation was around 4,500 feet. The air was noticeably cooler. Able to steer the motorcycle without hands, he removed the sweater and put it on. He wished he'd brought his flak jacket, but with the accident and resulting shock, it never entered his mind.

....

Manny was right. The trucks were moving through traffic, but not enough to be noticed. He'd made good time and now his Harley was a half-mile behind the two murderous hulks. He slowed when he saw them ahead, then checked the license plates through the binoculars. The rear truck's plates read AVW 732 PENNSYLVANIA.

I-10 East was a one way strip of highway paralleling I-10 West, also one way, with traffic coming in the opposite direction. The two freeways were separated by a patch of grass varying from fifty to two hundred fifty yards wide, depending upon terrain.

Steering with one hand, Manny swept the binoculars across the grassy knoll to I-10 westbound directly opposite his position, then scanned the westbound highway further ahead toward the east. Late afternoon traffic was heavy, but he could make out an army convoy speeding toward him, approximately two miles away.

....

The rapidly approaching convoy consisted of four Jeeps carrying soldiers with weapons, gas masks, and hand-held Chemical Agent Monitors (CAMS), one truck containing a squad of infantry, and a Spurpanzer Fuchs (Fox Reconnaissance Vehicle).

A unit of the National Guard in Las Cruces, after having been notified of the devastation at the Inspection Station on the border, had been ordered to investigate and search for the two trucks believed to be responsible heading east on I-10.

A radar transmitter mounted on the westbound Fox was bouncing signals off oncoming traffic approaching in the eastbound lane. At this point, the grassy knoll separating the two freeways was nearly one hundred yards wide.

In the lead Jeep, Major Vorhees, a small man with sharp features, was sitting beside his young Lieutenant, who was driving.

The CO had a vehicular mounted AN/VRQ3 radio in his Jeep. The Lieutenant, along with his duty as driver, was also the radio telephone operator. The CO hadn't been informed of the attacks on the Air Force Bases because the incoming communication from Base was garbled; all they could hear was a rushing noise.

"What's wrong with the damn radio transmission?" Major Vorhees demanded impatiently.

The Lieutenant glanced quickly at his commanding officer. "Sir, it's probably because there's too much advance on the SQUELCH control," he shouted above the roar of the radio static. "I need to readjust it. Also, the fact that we're not on high ground could be a factor."

"Fix the damn thing ASAP, Lieutenant! You know how important communication is, you shouldn't have let this happen!"

"Yes, sir! Sorry, sir. I'll take care of it."

Inside the body of the lead Super Truck, super computers were spitting out figures at a blinding speed, reacting to the radar scan from the approaching Fox. The screen changed color as the following data appeared:

INCOMING RADAR PROBE

I.D.:	Army Unit
APPROACH:	Westbound
GROUND/AIR:	Ground
SPEED:	70 Knots
UNIT:	Jeeps - 3
CONVOY TRUCK:	1
SPURPANZER FUCHS:	1

ARMOR PIERCING

CAPABILITY:	None
WEAPONRY:	Conventional,
M15	Assault Rifles.
12.7. mm	AA Machine Gun
DISTANCE:	3 Kilometers

....

In the lead Jeep, Major Vorhees was studying approaching traffic across the grassy area on the eastbound highway through binoculars. In the other two Jeeps, half a dozen soldiers were wearing gas masks and holding various weapons. In the lead truck, soldiers were sitting stiffly at attention holding their rifles ready, wearing gas masks. Bringing up the rear was the Fox Reconnaissance Vehicle.

Both the driver and his buddy were wearing biochemical gear.

....

In the eastbound lane, the trucks were closing fast on the convoy. In the rear Super Truck, a computer screen was printing out an update:

The "ATTACK MODE" option was blinking.

. . . .

As Manny knifed through traffic speeding east on I-10, he trained the binoculars on the convoy as it approached on I-10 West now a quarter of a mile away. He swept the binoculars back to the trucks on I-10 East ahead of him just as the two monsters pulled off the eastbound highway, crossed the grassy knoll, careened into the westbound lane going the wrong way, and headed straight for the convoy approaching on I-10 West.

Breen couldn't believe what he was seeing. "What the hell …?"

In the lead Jeep, Major Vorhees was looking through binoculars and also saw the trucks cross the knoll and head straight for them on I-10 West speeding against traffic.

"What the hell …?"

The trucks were rushing dead-on toward the convoy at over a hundred miles an hour. Oncoming westbound cars veered onto the shoulder to avoid the trucks, scattered off the highway onto the grassy knoll, several flipped upside down, then crashed into each other, caught fire and exploded as frantic drivers tried to evade the behemoths roaring toward them.

As the chaos grew, the rear truck pulled alongside the lead truck occupying both lanes of the two-lane highway. The only way to avoid a collision was for approaching traffic to swerve off the road onto the soft sand, a dangerous action at ninety-five mph.

A metal bar flipped up on each truck's front bumper; one bar telescoped into the other, joining them together forming a massive monolithic juggernaut. Electricity arced along the length of both trucks as they began pulsating with a soft light and quickly accelerated to a speed of one hundred twenty-five mph.

Major Vorhees was in shock. "They're crazy! They're —- WATCH OUT!"

Those were Vorhees' last words. As the trucks slammed into the convoy head on, a powerful negative magnetic force from the trucks repelled the lead Jeep, knocking it into the air, then the second and third Jeeps, which veered off the road and exploded.

Manny slowed, pulled over to the right shoulder, and stopped, letting the Harley idle. Glued to his binoculars, he watched as the trucks demolished the vehicle carrying the squad of men. The Fox Reconnaissance Vehicle, the only one left on the highway, began firing its 12.7 mm AA machine gun at the two destroyers. The rounds bounced harmlessly off their ceramic skin, causing small explosions. The two trucks repelled the Fox, which slammed into a passenger car; the car and the Fox burst into flames and flew into the air.

The battle was over in under thirty seconds.

After the carnage was complete, the trucks disengaged, slowed, then angled off the westbound highway, crossed the grass median, and casually reentered I-10 Eastbound.

. . . .

I-10 West was a war zone with smoking vehicles strewn for miles as ugly black smoke knifed into the grey afternoon sky like a surgeon's scalpel penetrating a cold cadaver. Secondary explosions ripped the Fox, sending debris spewing into the air.

Manny left the eastbound highway, crossed the grassy knoll and raced toward the wreckage of the lead Jeep. The Harley skidded to a stop as Breen surveyed the smoking wreckage. He slowly maneuvered the cycle past it to the second and third Jeeps, the army truck, and the demolished cars. There were no survivors.

He picked up a gas mask and CAM lying on the ground, then saw a body armor jacket obviously blown off an infantryman and secured it along with a pair of military dark glasses. He stopped momentari-ly, engine idling, long enough to put the glasses and jacket on. The jacket was just what he needed for warmth … and protection.

Manny gunned the engine, sliced across the grass back onto I-10 East, and sped after his targets.

………,

Port of Entry Inspection Station,
Arizona/New Mexico Border
2:30 p.m. Mountain Time

The area was swarming with police cars, ambulances, and fire trucks. An FBI chopper had just landed in the desert fifty yards from the station. The area had been cleared with CAMs brought in by the military.

Two men jumped from the aircraft and jogged toward the scene of devastation. One was Special Agent Don Baldwin, a big, mature African American, cynical and wary; the second man was Special Agent Koslowsky (Kos), young and eager, also tall with a charming smile.

The two men approached Sheriff Grundy who was standing outside the station speaking with Sharon Kramer.

Baldwin flashed his badge. "Special Agent Don Baldwin, FBI. This is Agent Jerry Koslowsky."

"I'm Sheriff Grundy," the Sheriff said, then, indicating Sharon, "this here's Sharon Kramer. She's a chopper pilot who's been followin' the trucks."

Baldwin looked skeptically at Sharon, a look she was used to being a woman in a man's world.

A trooper motioned Koslowsky over to his car a few feet away.

"I assume you've heard about the attacks on the Air Force Bases in New Mexico a half hour ago as well as the bases hit this morning in Arizona?" Baldwin said.

"Yeah, we were just talkin' about it. What the hell's goin' on?"

"We're sorting it out." Baldwin was still staring at Sharon. "So. What can you tell us about the trucks?"

"They're like oversized tanks. We saw 'em blow a police chopper out of the sky with a missile .."

Baldwin's eyes narrowed. "A missile? That explains how the bombs were delivered.   We think FAE's were used in all six attacks."

"My God!"

"Who's 'we'"?

"Detective Manny Breen, Phoenix P.D. The trucks killed his sister."

"Jesus. Where is he?"

"He's following the trucks."

Baldwin, who'd been surveying the damage, addressed the Sheriff.

"What kind of chemical agent did this?" Baldwin said.

"Won't know until the autopsies,' less we can get a Fox Spurpanzer out here from the army base."

Baldwin was wearing an earpiece. "What?" he said, lifting the microphone on his wrist to his mouth. "Fifteen minutes ago? Where, precisely?" He shook his head. "Uh, huh, Deming?" A beat, then, "Okay, we'll get over there!"

Baldwin addressed the Sheriff and Sharon. "A National Guard convoy was just destroyed near Deming by two trucks on I-10 West!"

As he was speaking, Agent Koslowsky, who'd overheard Baldwin's comment, left the trooper and hurried over. "That can wait. A trooper just informed me that the Air Force has made contact with the trucks near El Paso. Report is, the trucks were destroyed by two Warthogs!"

"Okay, let's go!" Agent Baldwin said, then, to Sharon, "Want to come?"

Sharon shrugged. "Is a Rabbi Jewish?"

Sharon and the agents ran to the chopper and got in as Sharon hopped in the rear seat. The Night Stalker lifted off, curved eastward, and quickly disappeared over the horizon.

....

Manny was speeding east on I-10 as several Long-bow Apaches screamed low overhead toward a heavy column of smoke.

As traffic clogged the road, Breen sliced over and sped east on the shoulder.

He slowed when he saw two burning trucks with black domes lying on their sides just off the highway. As Manny approached on the shoulder, two soldiers prevented him from entering the area.

"What happened?"

"We think they're the two trucks that destroyed that convoy back there …"

"Yeah," the other soldier said, "one of our Warthogs must have caught up with 'em …"

"Uh, huh," Manny said.

One of the soldiers noticed the gas mask on Manny's handlebars and saw the rifle. "Hey? Where'd you get the gas mask? What are you doing with that rifle?"

Manny flashed his badge. "I'm a Phoenix cop."

Breen revved the cycle, whipped around the soldiers and maneuvered the Harley close to the first burning truck. While he was inspecting it, Lt. Colonel Schultz sped up in a Jeep and screeched to a stop. He hopped out and drew his 45. "Hey! What do you think you're doing?"

Manny ignored the Lt. Colonel and cut over to the second truck. It was burning furiously and had a black dome similar to the super trucks.

As the Lt. Colonel and his men ran around the second truck yelling at him, Manny disappeared over a knoll as Schultz fired, missing him.

. . . .

Manny was driving slowly on the desert paralleling I-10 East studying the ground. He saw two sets of heavy tire tracks moving away from the highway and followed the tracks.

. . . .

Street In Front of Fazio's Manufacturing Plant In Phoenix
3:00 p.m. Mountain Time

A beat-up Ford pulled to a stop. Detectives Joey Payne and Chuck Ho peered through the car window at the plant.

"Okay," Joey said, "McDonnell Douglas checked out, let's try Fazio."

Inside the plant, a Supervisor led the two Detectives down a long corridor. They reached a glass partitioned office. The Supervisor stuck his head in.

"Mr. Kupchick, these detectives would like a word with you."

"Good day, gentlemen, come in," Kupchick said with a warm smile. He shook hands with the detectives, then ushered Payne and Ho into a plush office with photographs of trucks plastered on the walls.

"Please, sit down."

"That's okay, Mr. Kupchick, we just need a moment. I understand that Fazio Manufacturing Company does some work for the government?"

"Yes," Kupchick said, "our subsidiary on the east coast, Quanadine, is part of a consortium that builds the M1. That's the Abrams Tank."

"Uh, huh," Joey replied, "they use ceramic blocks for armor, don't they?"

Kupchick thought a moment. "I think so," he said.

Joey was looking through the partition at a man in the hall wearing a white smock. The man was a young, vital, Japanese American who seemed very agitated. He was talking to another man who kept checking his watch. After a few exchanges, the Asian threw his hands in the air and stalked away.

"I'm not an authority on that so forgive my vagueness. Sorry I can't be of more help."

"That's okay, thanks," Ho said.

Outside the office, the Asian and the man were back together, involved in a heated discussion. "Who's that?" Joey said, indicating the Asian in the hall.

Kupchick looked in the direction Joey indicated in time to see the Asian hurry away.

"Oh, that's Billy Oshiba. He's a computer genius Mr. Fazio uses from time to time. He's very excitable."

Joey and Chuck Ho got up to leave. Joey noticed a large photograph of a Marine on the wall.

"Your son?" Joey said.

"No, that's Mr. Fazio's son, Vincent, Jr. He was killed in the Gulf War. There's a photo of him in every office in the plant."

The detectives left the office and walked down the hall.

"I remember now, it was in the papers when his son died. There was a big flap about it …"

The detectives exited the plant and walked toward their car.

"… the kid was killed by friendly fire … Fazio was supposed to go to D.C. to receive a medal from the President for Vince, Jr. He told the President to go fuck himself."

Joey nodded. "Let's check it out."

. . . .

Located in Dona Ana County, the truck stop was on a flat, arid plateau, with various peaks and mesas visible in the distance, including Picacho Peak.

Manny pulled into the truck stop on the Harley and slowed. At least twenty-five trucks were parked near the gas pumps. On the other side of I-10 was a vegetable stand.

Breen sat for a moment on the Harley, engine idling, warily studying the trucks. The tire imprints in the sand had led to this location.

He decided to visit the diner first, then check out the parked trucks.

Manny headed for a gas pump and filled the Harley, tied his gas mask to the cycle, stuck the CAM under his jacket, wheeled the motorcycle to a parking place, then hid his rifle in some nearby bushes.

After one more look at the trucks and the vegetable stand across the highway, he headed for the diner. On the way in, he made note of the cars parked in front of the restaurant, including a Chevy, an Olds, two beat-up pickup trucks, and a Honda.

………

It was a small, tacky restaurant with half a dozen tables and a counter. A juke box was playing Billy Joel's "River Of Dreams". Manny loved the song that had just hit number three on the pop chart. He even liked the album cover painted by Joel's wife, Christie Brinkley.

Breen sat at the counter, ordered a Coke and a burger with fries. While he was waiting, he casually checked the diner's customers.

A man dressed in coveralls was sitting at one of the tables with his wife. Their clothes suggested they were local farmers in their late sixties. A hefty woman in her thirties was seated at another table with a crying infant, and there where three men dressed in slacks with open shirts in their thirties who looked out of place. All three were beefy, in great shape, athletic looking, and several kept checking something outside through the large plate glass window. They definitely were not truckers.

After Breen finished his burger, he realized how hungry he was and ordered a second take-out. While waiting for the order, he went into the bathroom, locked himself in a stall, and checked out his Glock 22.

First manufactured in 1990, the Glock was the most reliable handgun Manny had used. With a 15 round capacity and a safe-action trigger, the weapon could deliver between four hundred twenty and five hundred foot-pounds of kinetic energy. The weapon fit nicely into Manny's Johnny Ringo Leather Holster and Gun Belt and with the two extra round mags he carried in his pocket, he'd never been caught short in a gun fight.

Breen loved the holster; it was fashioned from the 1993 movie, "Tombstone," and gave the detective a quick draw. He'd also had a secret pouch sewn into the inside of his belt where he could keep vital pieces of information. The weapon itself was concealed underneath the bullet-proof jacket he'd acquired.

Manny also carried a backup .38 on his ankle.

After checking the chamber and relieving himself, Manny returned to the diner, picked up his order, threw some bills on the counter, and headed for the door.

Outside the diner, he passed the Honda and noticed two men sitting inside the car sipping coffee. Manny thought nothing of it and walked to the other side of the gas pumps where the trucks were parked.

A large eighteen wheeler with a black dome was too obvious. He strolled casually past it, took the CAM out of his jacket, and trained it on the truck. The Chemical Agent Monitor did not respond.

After checking the rest of the trucks without success, he looked around, puzzled. A large truck was sitting apart from the others. It had the words, "A Moving Experience" written on the sides. Then Manny remembered flying over a truck with those words printed on it when he first teamed up with Sharon in the chopper. He made a mental note and thought it was either a coincidence or that the truck belonged to an organization with lots of commercial vehicles on the road and this was part of the fleet. It wasn't disguised and he knew it wasn't one of the two trucks.

Manny paused. He was sure he was in the right place. All indications were that the trucks had come this way, and if they were here, somehow they were being disguised. He glanced across the road at the vegetable stand and noticed a huge tarp covering a structure behind the stand.

Breen crossed I-10. A large, extremely muscular African American was standing under the awning behind the counter. He reminded Manny of body builder Victor Richards.

"Where's your neck?" Manny said, taking an apple.

The big guy stared at him but said nothing. Manny checked the vegetable stand's interior, saw nothing unusual, pulled out some change and tossed it on the counter.

He was about to return to the diner across the highway on I-10 when a sixth sense stopped him. Curious, he walked around to the side of the stand.

The tarpaulin was covering a huge object. Then something drew Manny's eye; the tarp was caught on a large tire. His pulse jumped dramatically. Careful not to get too close, he checked to see if anyone was watching, then carefully took the CAM of of his pocket and trained it on the tarp. The CAM's sensor went berserk. Suddenly, the hidden trucks' engines roared as the "vegetable stand" started to move down the road.

Simultaneously, the three men burst out of the diner and sprinted across I-10 to the vegetable stand as the beefy guy scrambled out from under the collapsing awning being dragged behind the trucks. Vegetables were scattering everywhere.

"*SHIT*!" one of the guys shouted at no-neck as the three ran up, "What happened?"

"The trucks knew they were being scanned," the no-neck guy shouted, jamming Manny's shoulder. "This guy did it! You almost got me killed, you asshole!"

"I'll never forgive myself," Manny replied, backing away from all four men. The no-neck guy took a step forward, then jammed Manny's shoulder again. "That hurts," Breen said with a pained look.

"Yeah? How does this feel?" The guy threw a punch. Manny moved slightly to the side and with one move knocked him flat.

Two of the thugs went for their guns, one pulled a knife; in a split second, all three were slightly heavier, each with a 180 grain Full Metal Jacket bullet in a vital organ from Manny's Glock.

When no-neck, still on the ground, pulled his weapon, Breen shot him in the heart.

Manny glanced down the road, saw the trucks speeding away, quickly rifled through the pockets of the dead and dying men. On one, he found a single gold key; on another, a dog-eared map. He put the key and the map in his jacket pocket, zipped it up, and grabbed an automatic weapon one of the men was carrying.

Breen tucked his Glock back in his holster and raced across the road toward his motorcycle in time to see two teenagers snatch the gas mask from the Harley and run off.

"HEY …!" Manny yelled, but it was too late. In an instant, he was on the Harley flying down I-35 … twenty-two seconds later, the battle began.

………

In his initial encounter with the two demons, Manny had been at a disadvantage driving a car. With the Harley, he had greater agility, more maneuverability, and he presented a smaller, swifter target. The odds were still against him, but they were vastly improved.

The trucks were moving east on I-10 single file at over a hundred mph. Manny closed quickly, sped past traffic and came up on the right shoulder at a hundred twenty.

Armed with a powerful gun, he'd only glanced at the automatic weapon he'd snatched back at the truck stop, but Manny had instantly identified it as a Calico M960 submachine gun. It fed from a helical magazine fitted over the receiver.

Acutely aware of the trucks' super defenses, he had one advantage: The element of surprise. For cover, he stayed behind a conventional truck following monster trucks, then zipped around the truck on the shoulder, sped up beside the rear Super Truck, fired a quick burst of automatic fire at the truck's rear tires, instantly braked and ducked back behind the conventional truck, narrowly avoiding a burst of machine gun fire from the rear truck's defensive posture.

Manny's attack had no effect on the tires. Realizing he couldn't affect the trucks' tires, Breen's next strategy was to use the trucks against them-selves.

Again, he whipped out from behind the conventional truck and passed the rear truck at high speed, this time on the outside (left) lane, then swerved between the two juggernauts, sandwiched between the lead truck by only a few feet and the rear truck not more than six feet behind him.

When he glanced back and saw the rear truck speed up to crush him between the two vehicles, he darted out of the way causing the rear truck to ram its sister.

Again, there was no damage to the Goliaths.

Now speeding off the highway on the desert left of and paralleling the trucks, Manny saw the lead Super Truck's side-panel slide up. Fearing another heat-seeking missile, he braked, zoomed back on the highway, cutting dangerously close behind the rear Super Truck, and cut across I-10 to the right shoulder, evading the missile that zoomed across the grassy knoll and obliterated a truck traveling west on the I-10 westbound corridor.

When they entered a tunnel, the shoulder suddenly vanished; Manny found himself between the rear truck and the wall of the tunnel. When the truck swerved over to try to crush him against the wall, Breen instantly braked, dropping behind the truck with the result that it rammed into the cement, causing damage to the rear truck's right door handle.

As they shot out of the tunnel, the rear Super Truck emitted a brilliant flash of light just as Manny swerved back onto the right shoulder. This time, his dark military glasses, especially fitted for extreme brightness, mitigated the effect. Still traveling on the right shoulder, Manny shot past the rear truck and moved parallel with the lead truck firing a burst at the cab; again the rounds bounced off, causing small explosions.

Manny looked up. He was fast approaching a construction project five hundred feet ahead. He made a snap decision, took the up-ramp to the unfinished highway a level above that paralleled I-10 East, and now was slightly ahead of the two trucks to their right looking down on them forty feet below.

The dreadnoughts began firing missiles at the new highway above them, demolishing each section of the new road behind Manny as he cleared each one. His speed: a hundred thirty mph! Suddenly, he saw the construction of the upper level was about to end. Manny made another snap decision, soared off the upper ramp, and landed the Harley on the roof of the lead truck.

The motorcycle skidded off the truck, slammed onto the highway behind him and was crushed underneath the rear truck, but Breen held on to the edge of the roof. He looked inside the truck's cab. The vehicle was driverless.

Breen pulled himself up as the top of the truck began to glow red hot. The trucks had slowed at a railroad crossing. As his shoes started to smoke, Manny jumped off, landing on the sand near the shoulder. He rolled over, then jumped to his feet as the trucks bore down on him.

There was a pond on the side of the road, a hundred feet away. Could he could make it? Manny sprinted faster than a magnet attracts metal, jumped into the pond and swam to the center with the trucks close on his heels. He treaded water as the two monsters waited, obviously calculating their next move. Whomever had programmed the leviathans hadn't written this scenario into their code.

After a beat, the trucks began slowly circling the pond like Native Americans circling a wagon train.

Suddenly a fuel tank rolled out from underneath one of the tracks into the pond, floating lazily toward Manny. A side panel slid up on the front truck and a flamethrower spit out a stream of liquid fire.

Manny took a deep breath, then dove beneath the water as the fuel tank exploded, sending a sheet of liquid flame across the pond that quickly became a roaring inferno.

Swimming underwater in a bulletproof jacket was impossible, so he discarded it. Breen stayed underwater for several minutes, then surfaced under a dock. Manny threw water on the flames around him and managed to find a breathing space.

The trucks waited as fire ravaged the pond … then slowly moved away, disappearing over the rise. Manny emerged from under the dock, now totally engulfed in flames, and climbed onto the shore. He looked for and found his soleless shoes, put them on anyway and limped off after the trucks.

……….

Fazio's Mansion In Tucson Arizona
4:30 p.m. Mountain Time

This was the home of a multi-billionaire; massive manicured lawns, statues in cleverly arranged pools, flowers and trees placed in artful patterns in a Japanese garden, and then the mansion itself. It stretched over half an acre, was three stories high with twenty bedrooms, an indoor swimming pool and marble imported from Italy making the floors patchwork patterns of mosaic beauty.

Joey Payne and Chuck Ho were sitting on the edge of the couch in a spacious living room featuring original Van Goghs and other works of art on the walls, speaking to Mrs. Fazio, an attractive, mature woman in her early sixties.

Joey and Chuck Ho were both holding glasses of ice cold lemonade.

"Thanks for seeing us, Mrs. Fazio," Joey said. "Has your husband been acting strange lately or …"

"Vincent moved out over a year ago. I haven't seen him since."

"Oh," Joey said, nodding.

"After our son was killed, Vincent was never the same. He blamed the President, the Air Force … at the cemetery, he just stared into space …it was filmed."

"Do you have a copy of that tape, Mrs. Fazio?"

"No, but I have the clippings you asked for."

Mrs. Fazio picked up a portfolio from the coffee table and handed it to Joey.

Detective Ho saw a photograph on the table and picked it up. It was a photo of Fazio at his desk at the CIA surrounded by his buddies. "This your husband?"

"Yes," Mrs. Fazio said. "Those are some of his friends in the CIA."

Joey looked up. "He was in the CIA?"

"Yes, for thirty years."

Joey glanced at Ho. They got up to leave.

"Thanks for seeing us, Mrs. Fazio," Joey said, "and we're deeply sorry for your loss."

"Thank you, you're very gracious," Mrs. Fazio said.

....

Once inside the car, they sat looking at the newspaper clippings.

"Okay," Joey said, "here's the scenario. Fazio's son is killed by friendly fire. He goes ape and vows to get revenge. He just happens to be a billionaire with CIA connections …"

"… and just happens to be a truck manufacturer with a knowledge of how to build trucks," Ho continued.

"… and how to plot their movements with satellite tracking systems …"

"So he builds these two super monsters and turns 'em loose on the Air Force."

Joey nodded. "Let's go to the TV station."

Ho nodded. "Good idea."

As they drove away, Joey continued. "Let's check out Billy Oshiba."

Ho looked at him. "You mean me, right?"

Joey shrugged. "Only if you want to."

....

Local Highway 70 Near Las Cruces
6:50 p.m. Mountain Time

Breen was sitting on a rock, studying the map he'd taken from Fazio's men. It had a series of areas circled. At the top of the map scrawled in longhand was the following data:

Truck 1 (55661367)
Truck 2 (93711921)

Manny was shivering. The temperature was in the forties but the pond had felt like ice. He forced the cold out of his mind, committed the numbers and locations to memory, then examined the gold key. After removing his belt and turning it over, Manny unzipped the secret compartment and slipped the key inside. It was then he noticed that his Glock and .38 were missing. He'd either lost them when he landed on top of the truck or when he was in the pond. Breen stuffed the map back in his pocket, zipped it up, and headed for the nearby local highway.

. . . .

Road Leading To Local Highway
7:10 p.m. Mountain Time

It was getting dark. Manny was jogging along the road, lifting his knees high and swinging his arms to keep warm, when a car approached from behind. He stuck out his thumb; the car, a late model Honda, slowed and stopped. Manny walked up as John Jamington Fryer rolled the window down.

"Get in."

"Thanks," Manny said as he hopped in the back seat.

J.J. was observing him through the rearview mirror. "Where you headed?"

"I-20," Manny replied.

"So are we," J.J. said. "Got off to look for a restaurant we heard about near Roscoe and got lost. How'd you get wet?"

"It's a long story. Made a wrong turn, ended up in a cow pond."

J.J. laughed. "Too bad. We've got an extra jacket back there, you're free to use it."

Thanks," Manny said, found the item and put it on.

"You look familiar. Didn't we see you back at the truck stop?"

Manny nodded. "Yeah, I stopped to get gas and make a pit stop."

"Uh, huh," J.J. said, still studying him in the mirror.

They rode in silence a moment. "Heard anything about these two trucks?"

"What trucks?"

"Where you from?"

Manny hesitated. "The southeast."

J.J.glanced at Fazio who pulled a .45 out, turned and pointed it at Manny's head.

"We think you're lying," Fazio said. "We think you're the cop from Phoenix we've been hearing about on the radio, the same cop who killed four of our men. Let me see your hands."

....

Detectives Joey Payne and Chuck Ho were sitting in a viewing room in front of a large TV screen watching footage of Fazio's interview at the cemetery. On the screen, a reporter had just mentioned to Fazio that he'd been invited to the White House to receive the Silver Star for his son, Vincent, Jr.

Vincent's response had been explosive. "The sons-of-bitches who killed my boy will pay! I'm going to the White House all right, but not to get a fucking piece of metal!" Fazio lunged at the screen as it went blank.

Joey took out the Police Artist's sketch given them by the motorist who survived the service station massacre.

"Looks like him, right?"

"I'd say so," Ho replied.

Joey thought a moment. "Question: If you wanted to build a couple of killer trucks under the radar, where would you do it?"

"Some place where nobody could watch."

"Like the desert?"

"Yep."

"Okay," Joey said, "let's make some calls."

A Farm House And Barn Near Las Cruces
8:15 p.m. Mountain Time

The Honda pulled up and parked outside the boarded up farmhouse. Fazio and J.J. got out, motioned Manny out with their guns drawn and entered the farmhouse, forcing Manny before them.

The living room was laid out like a Command Center. On the wall was a huge map of the United States. The route along I-10 East leading to I-20 was illuminated. Flags were stuck in areas around the highway route designating refueling stations and AFB targets, the final destination being Washington, D.C. which was in red.

Two blinking lights indicated the trucks' current location in the barn outside.

Several of Fazio's men were standing in front of the map as another man, Snake Scopec, was sitting at the dining room table talking on the phone. Scopec was big and ugly.

Fazio and J.J. entered, pushing Manny inside.

"Check this guy out," Fazio said as two of the men grabbed Manny and began searching him.

Scopec hung up and walked over to Fazio holding a notepad.

"What's the kill rate?" Fazio said.

Scopec checked the notepad. "Early estimates from all six bases are around eighty-five hundred. White Sands alone was over three thousand."

Fazio smiled. "When we hit Dyess Air Force Base, we should reach ten-thousand."

One of the men handed him Manny's detective badge and the map.

Fazio looked at the map, then at Manny. "You got this map from one of our boys at the truck stop, didn't you?"

Manny didn't answer. Fazio slapped him hard across the face.

"Find out what he knows. Don't kill him yet."

Three of the men grabbed Manny and headed for the door. Manny stopped and turned back.

"Since I'm about to die, tell me your objective."

A beat. Fazio smiled. "Let's just say it'll be a moving experience."

The men pushed Manny out the door.

....

I-10 East At Site Of The Burning Trucks
8:30 p.m. Mountain Time

It was early evening when an FBI chopper curved around and landed in the desert not far from the burning trucks. Agent Baldwin hopped out, followed by Sharon and Agent Kos. The Lt. Colonel who confronted Manny approached as Baldwin flashed his badge.

"Agent Baldwin, FBI," Baldwin said, looking at the burning trucks.

"Who nailed these babies?"

"We think it was one of our Warthogs got 'em," the Lt. Colonel responded. Baldwin looked back at the Colonel. "But you don't know for sure."

"Not yet."

Baldwin looked at Sharon who was studying the trucks. "Look familiar?"

Sharon took her time before answering. "I can't tell." She addressed the Lt. Colonel. "You didn't happen to see a guy on a Harley, did you?"

"Yeah, I took a shot at him."

Sharon's penetrating focus on the Colonel was withering. "I hope you missed, soldier. That was a Phoenix detective."

The Lt. Colonel shrugged. "He was acting suspicious, drove over that rise." He pointed to the
slightly sloping hill to the north.

. . . .

Men could be heard working on the trucks in the main area of the barn.

Manny was hanging by his feet from an overhead beam illuminated by a spotlight mounted on the wall. His hands were tied behind his back.

Three men were standing around him. Manny's head was level with theirs. These three hefty guys had been recruited from the Irish Mafia. Not trained in martial arts, they were still brutal and formidable opponents in a fight. Brothers, their names were Mick, Bobby, and Johnny.

Mick, the tallest of the three stepped closer to Manny and shoved his face within inches of Breen's head. "Where'd you get the map? Tell us what you know, we'll kill you quick."

"I don't like my options," Manny said, and slammed his head into Mick's face. Mick went down hard.

Mick sat on the cement floor, stunned. He slowly looked up at Breen. "Jesus! You-son-of a … I'm gonna kill you now, you asshole …!"

Bobby hit Manny in the ribs as Mick hopped up and smashed him in the face. Manny groaned.

"You like that, motherfucker?" Mick yelled.

"Take it easy," Johnny said, "you kill him now, Fazio'll feed you to the Jolly Green Giant in the truck." He stepped up to Manny. "How much do the authorities know about the trucks?"

Manny was swinging back and forth from the blows. He took a beat, then said, "What trucks?"

. . . .

The main area of the barn was a high-tech shop with state-of-the-art equipment. The trucks were being overhauled by a squad of mechanics being overseen by Billy Oshiba.

Two men wearing goggles were using blow-torches to repair the handle of the second truck damaged in the battle with Breen as another worker approached the first truck whose back panel was up. As he did so, the protective badge he was wearing fell to the ground. The worker didn't notice and entered the rear of the truck.

The truck's interior was a mass of computers in the front of the truck and weapon systems throughout the main body. A warning light began blinking over a panel near the rear of the truck marked

LAST RESORT.

A panel door slid up. A huge, faceless robot stood recessed in the wall. Its eyes began to glow.

The worker was standing with his back to the robot, adjusting one of the weapon systems. Suddenly he sensed something behind him and turned as the robot grabbed his right arm, then his left arm, and pulled him apart.

Outside in the shop the mechanics heard the worker scream as both his arms came flying out of the truck, then his head. A mechanic noticed the protective badge on the ground and picked it up.

Oshiba hurried over. "What happened?"

He held out the badge. "Looks like Carl's protective badge fell off."

Oshiba took the badge and made an announcement. "I'll say it again; be extremely careful when working around these trucks. Without your badge, this is what can happen!" He waved the badge in the air.

....

Manny was still hanging upside down; the brothers were taking turns pounding him as Fazio stuck his head in.

"Anything?"

"No," Mick said, panting.

"I didn't think so. He's a cop, he's too stupid to save his life. Take him out behind the barn and kill him." Fazio left the stall as Mick cut Manny down.

"Let's have a party," Mick said, staring at Manny. "Get a few more of the guys. This fucker doesn't deserve an easy death."

Mick and Bobby pulled Breen to his feet and forced him out of the stall into the main area of the barn. As they were walking toward the door leading to the outside, Manny observed an Asian in a white coat as the brothers pushed him to the rear door.

. . . .

The night was cold, clear and crisp with a slight wind. Floodlights on top of the barn illuminated a circular area on the ground outside the barn. Farm equipment was sitting against a side of the barn along with a tractor, a bale of hay, and a tillage machine. Manny was pushed through the door followed by the brothers and three other henchmen who'd joined the "party."

The men threw Manny into the center of the light and circled him.

Breen's hands were still tied behind his back. Mick stepped forward.

"We're going to beat you to death, asshole. Got anything to say?"

"Good luck," Manny said. He looked around the circle of his attackers as they started to close in. Suddenly, Manny leapt high in the air, pulled his knees to his chest and with one deft move, swung his clenched fists beneath his feet. This time he made it, landing successfully with his tied hands in front of him.

Manny had been preparing all his life for this moment. He'd always known there would come a test, one he'd have to meet, greater than those before. Although he'd been badly beaten, from his vast experience in the martial arts, he was inured to pain. His confidence in his ability to meet this challenge was supreme.

Shutting out all external phenomena, he took two deep breaths, then focused on the strategy he would use to defeat his captors. There were six enemy combatants of different size and strength. The Phoenix cop had excellent peripheral vision which gave him an advantage. He quickly analyzed the distance between each attacker. The ones close together would be easier to manage.

Breen had no doubt he would triumph; the only question was: could he accomplish it in ten moves.

Mick was the first to attack. As he approached, Manny kicked him in the knee, breaking it, then chopped him in the throat on his way down, crushing his Adam's apple.

One of the three invitees to the "party" was martial arts trained. He jumped in the air and tried to kick Manny, but Breen caught his leg, broke it, then threw his tied hands around the man's neck, snapping it with one powerful move.

Johnny and Bobby attacked from different angles, one with a knife. Manny swiftly sidestepped Johnny, grabbed him and whirled him around. When Bobby's knife thrust caught Johnny in the gut fatally wounding him, Breen delivered a blow to Bobby's temple with his elbow. Bobby was dead before he hit the ground.

There were two men still standing. One went for his gun as Manny somersaulted to him before he could fire, kicked him in the crotch, then broke his arm, then his neck.

The last man grabbed a pitchfork and charged as Breen sidestepped him, snatched the pitchfork from his hands and shoved it through his abdomen.

The condensed fight had taken less than twenty seconds; it was short but deadly. Manny counted twelve moves. He'd have to settle for that.

Breen picked up the knife, cut the ropes freeing his hands, and took a weapon from one of the dead men. He was about to run when he noticed a protective badge on one of Fazio's men, came back, removed it, then sprinted toward a patch of woods fifty yards away as two more of Fazio's contingent ran from the barn shooting at him.

Manny returned their fire and made it to the woods. As he looked back, he saw another man emerge from the barn with a hand-held missile launcher.

"Aw, shit!" Manny cursed, then ran like hell as the man fired the MANPAD at him. The missile blew a hole in some trees as Manny came out the other side of the woods and kept going.

·········

Fazio was talking on the phone in the Command Center. "Sell it! Sell everything, convert to cash, I want it all in my Swiss accounts as soon as the banks open in the morning …"

The man with the missile launcher ran in. "Mr. Fazio, that cop got away, he killed …"

Fazio was finishing up on the phone. "Do it, Mike!" He slammed the receiver down and looked at the man. "Slow down, start over."

The man was breathless, breathing hard. "That cop … he, shit, he killed everybody!"

Fazio gave the man a cold stare. "All six?"

The man nodded. "Yeah, all six."

More cold stares. "And did you say he got away?"

"Yeah, I got off a shot, but I couldn't find his body."

Without hesitation, Fazio shot the guy in the heart.

J.J., standing nearby, had observed the action.

"Looks like I underestimated Mr. Breen. It doesn't matter." Fazio stuck his Sig Sauer back in its shoulder holster, then addressed J.J. who was approaching. "We'll fly ahead and wait for the van in Arlington." He made an announcement to the rest of his team. "Listen up! Proceed as planned. Nothing's changed … Good luck!"

....

On a hill overlooking the barn, Manny watched as the trucks emerged and moved off down a dirt road toward the local highway. He limped off after them.

....

Local Highway Near Highway 70
9:10 p.m. Mountain Time

Manny was walking east along the highway when a state police car sped by, jammed on the brakes, stopped, and backed up. Two State Police Troopers got out.

"You Manny Breen?" Trooper Brian said.

"Yeah."

"Get in, the FBI wants you in Dallas," Gonzales, the other trooper, said.

Manny looked at him. "I don't have time." Manny started to walk away.

"If you're still after the trucks, forget it, they're history," Trooper Brian said.

Manny looked back. "You think so, huh?" He continued down the road as Trooper Gonzales pulled his gun.

"HOLD IT, BREEN!" he ordered.

Manny stopped and looked at the trooper. "You going to shoot me?"

"Miguel, put the gun away," Trooper Brian said, then to Manny, "Nobody's going to shoot you. Look. Come in with us, you're a mess. You can get some food and, I don't know, maybe some shoes that work."

Breen looked at his shattered shoes, shrugged, and got in the car with the troopers.

Trooper Brian picked up the radio mic. "This is 2510 …"

The dispatcher's voice came on. "Go ahead, 2510 …"

Trooper Brian looked at Manny. "What's your shoe size?"

"10-C."

"Call the FBI in Dallas. Tell 'em Breen's on his way in. And he needs a pair of shoes, 10-C …

"Right," the dispatcher said, "pair of shoes. Imported?"

"Yeah," Trooper Brian said, "two-tone …"

……….

Phoenix Police Department, Homicide Division
8:10 a.m. Mountain Time

Joey was at his desk flipping through the scrapbook given to them by Mrs. Fazio as Ho looked over his shoulder.

"The kid was only twenty. Joined the Marines in '89, got killed in '91."

Ho nodded. "What was the precise time he was killed?"

"It doesn't say."

"What was the date on those leaflets dropped on the White House?"

"Don't ask me," Joey said, closing the book.

"I'll make make some calls," Det. Ho said, heading to his desk as Joey's phone rang.

"Payne, Homicide." He stopped reading and looked up. "Yeah?" Joey made a note on a pad. "Where?" More writing. "Yeah, thanks." He hung up as Det. Ho came over.

"Got something?"

"Hang glider saw a burned out building in the desert just north of Quartzsite. I'm going to check it out." He ripped the paper out and headed for the door.

"Call Frank Weiler at the FBI in Phoenix," Joey said to Ho. "Tell 'im we may have something on those trucks. We'll need a chopper. I'll meet him on the pad in twenty minutes."

As Joey was leaving, Chief Hunt entered. "Where you going?"

"The John. Got a bad taco last night," Joey said, walking out the door.

The Chief looked at Ho. "I thought he was a vegetarian."

"He is. It was a taco with Brussels sprouts."

....

Desert Ten Miles North Of Quartzsite, Arizona
9:50 a.m. Mountain Time

An FBI chopper was circling the area. Inside were Joey Payne and Agent Weiler, a tall, beefy square-jawed young man who could play Superman.

The remains of the isolated warehouse were apparent in the desert below. The chopper dropped down and flew low over the structure, then circled back and hovered over the tire tracks leading across the sand. Joey was studying the tracks through binoculars.

The pilot made contact with base. "This is Zebra Nine to Charlie Five. Do you read me?"

"This is Charlie Five," the voice responded, "go ahead Zebra Nine."

The pilot was studying the building below. "Have a burned out warehouse about five miles southwest of Bumble Bee off I-17. Looks like tire tracks on the dirt road leading away from it."

"Roger that, Zebra Nine."

"Copy, ten four."

The chopper turned and headed south back to the Station.

....

Desert Near The Burnt Out Warehouse
10:35 a.m. Mountain Time

A dozen police cars from the Phoenix P.D., several plain-looking Buicks and some Arizona State Police sped across the desert and kicked up sand as they slid to a stop in front of the warehouse.

Immediately the FBI and police swarmed over the area searching the ruins, sifting gingerly through the wreckage. Several steel girder supports were still standing, giving the building an eerie, skeletal appearance.

Joey and Ho, wearing gloves, were checking the area when Joey spied something the size of a nickel in the ruins, picked it up and turned it over.

"HEY!" Joey shouted, "I THINK I FOUND SOMETHING!"

Agent Weiler and the others hurried over. "What is this?" Joey said, holding the object between his fingers.

Weiler took it and examined it closely. "I don't know," he said, turning the object over. "We'll have our munitions experts check it out."

....

The FBI was born in 1905 under the sharp eye and stern law and order enforcement of Teddy Roosevelt. The new organization's mission: handle investigations for the Department of Justice.

The organization was jostled from pillar to post for nearly one hundred years until finally, in 2002, it found its current home.

Sharon Kramer was talking to Joey Payne, Agent Baldwin, and Agent Weiler in a private office of the FBI building when Manny walked in carrying a new pair of shoes.

"Joey!" Manny said with a big smile. "What are you doing here?"

Joey ran up to Manny and hugged him. "How you doing, amigo? What's with the shoes?"

"Outgrew 'em," Manny said, then to Sharon, "We have to talk, but first I have to call Phoenix."

"Use this phone," Baldwin said, showing Manny to a desk. Baldwin took Joey aside. "Come on, Payne, let's compare notes."

Joey left with Agent Baldwin as Manny sat down at the desk and dialed a number.

"Want some coffee?" Sharon said.

"Yeah," then into the receiver, "Charlie, this is Manny. I need you to make funeral arrangements … you have? I appreciate that … yeah, thanks, I'll be back in a day or two." Manny hung up.

Sharon took his hand. "Come on."

She lead him to the coffee machine and poured a cup. "What happened to your shoes?"

"The trucks gave me a hot foot."

"I explained to the Harley's owner at the diner why you "borrowed" his bike. Told him not to worry."

"He should have worried."

Sharon smiled. "It's history, right?"

Manny nodded. "Yeah."

Sharon watched him sip the coffee. "You had any sleep?"

"Yeah, I got some last year."

"Everyone's convinced the trucks were destroyed."

"Those were decoys."

Sharon took out a Kleenex and wiped a smudge off Manny's forehead. They looked at each other. Manny's eyes filled with tears. Sharon put her hand on his cheek.

"Don't be nice to me."

Sharon smiled as Agent Baldwin stuck his head in the door. "Okay, everybody in the conference room!"

....

Private Conference Room, FBI
2:05p.m. Central Time

Manny, Sharon, Joey, Weiler, Lt. Col. Schultz and Baldwin were seated at the circular conference table along with Sonny McGuire. McGuire was a big, rugged man who could have played guard for the New York Giants. He hadn't smiled in twenty years.

"I'm Sonny McGuire," McGuire began, "FBI Chief of Operations for the southwest. We're in a national crisis. Six Air Force Bases have been hit in the past twelve hours. We have investigative teams at all six locations. So far, the military believes they were attacked by FAE's delivered by air, probably low-flying missiles. What was the means of delivery? We're exploring every possibility." He paused, looked around the table and picked up a folder on the table in front of him. "I want as much information as you can give me on these two so-called death trucks tearing up jack on I-10. Frankly, I'm skeptical of what I'm reading in this report."

Manny stared at him. "Yeah? Why is that?"

"Other than a few questionable eye-witness reports, there's no credible evidence of their existence. How could a truck, two trucks, fire missiles, dispense poisonous gas, have state-of-the art armor ceramic plating and weapon systems that can deliver FAEs and chemical warheads? Do you know the cost it would take to plan and develop something like this? Why should I believe that these trucks are responsible for the attacks?"

Manny's impatience was growing. "Because I've seen them in action."

"They blew a police helicopter out of the sky and barely missed my chopper with a missile," Sharon added.

"How do you know it wasn't automatic weapon's fire? And who are you? And you?" McGuire stated abruptly with a hint of condescension, indicating both Sharon and Manny.

Manny was ready to walk. "She knows the difference, McGuire, she was in Desert Storm!"

"So was Manny," Joey said, chiming in, "he was a gunnery sergeant, won a bunch of medals."

"You don't have to defend me to this asshole, Joey, I don't have time for this bullshit!" Manny headed for the door.

"HOLD IT, BREEN!" McGuire shouted. Manny stopped at the door.

"This could all be a moot point. According to this report," McGuire said, continuing, "the trucks have been neutralized." He nodded to Col. Schultz. "Shultz?"

"That's what we believe, Chief," Lt. Col. Schultz said, "we believe the two trucks burning out of control on I-10 were the ones responsible for attacking the army convoy."

Manny turned on Schultz. "You're an idiot, Schultz, those were decoys. After you took that pot shot at me, I found the trucks, the real ones. Believe me, they're out there and they're lethal…!" Then, to McGuire, "…. and how they got made and why they have such advanced weapon systems and how they navigate driverless, I don't know, but I do know they're responsible for the attacks!"

"There haven't been any incidents since the destruction of those two "decoys," McGuire insisted with a sarcastic twist on the word.

"Yeah,?" Breen said, "well, get ready. Their next target is Dyess Air Force Base near Abilene!"

Baldwin stood up. "Breen? Can you I.D. this?" He tossed the object they'd found in the desert to Manny.

Breen looked at the object, rolling it over in his hands. "It's an impeller," Breen said, "it increases the kill-zone of a shell by allowing it to explode above the ground."

"We found it in the ruins of a demolished structure ten miles north of Quartzsite on a plateau in the desert," Baldwin said to the Chief. "We think it's the secret facility used to build the trucks."

McGuire looked at Manny. "How do you know they're going to hit Dyess?"

"I read it in a fortune cookie." Manny started out as an agent stuck his head in the door .

"Dyess Air Force Base has just been hit with a chemical warhead!"

"Period!" Manny stated, then strode through the door followed by Baldwin.

"How's that guy get off being an asshole?" Breen said as they headed for the hall. "He's not even a lawyer!"

Baldwin laughed as Sharon and Joey exited the conference room behind them.

. . . .

Manny and crew moved briskly down the corridor.

"The trucks should be refueling at an Exxon station east of Tyler, Texas in about three hours," Manny said.

Baldwin looked at him. "How do you know?"

"I saw a map. It had refueling stops circled, and in the corner were two code numbers — I think they're the trucks' access codes. I also have this …" Breen stopped, removed his belt, and produced the gold key. "Took it off a dead terrorist."

Joey gave a photo to Manny. "Recognize this guy?"

After a quick glance, Manny nodded. "Yeah, that's the guy in charge of the whole operation."

"Name's Vincent Fazio," Baldwin said, "his son was killed by friendly fire in Desert Storm. Guess how he made his billions?"

"Trucks," Manny replied.

"You got it!"

"He's been following the trucks in a Honda with D.C. plates."

"He's ex-CIA, has lots of buddies still in the Agency," Baldwin said, then looked at Sharon. "Want to do some flying?"

Sharon shrugged. "Does a baby suck its thumb?"

....

Farmhouse Where The Trucks Were Repaired
3:00 p.m. Mountain Time

State Police and FBI were everywhere searching for evidence. They entered the house and barn … both were empty, wiped clean of any evidence, as if someone had just committed a crime and attempted to remove all the evidence.

………

Billy Oshiba was a Hafu, a child born of a non-Japanese mother. She was Asian, his father Japanese. Being Hafu had been a stigma growing up in his native country and made him feel like an outsider from the start.

Then there was his I.Q. Some are considered exceptionally bright at 150, but because Billy was 'different' than other children and could solve the Genius Cube in one minute, his parents decided to have him tested. When it was discovered his I.Q. was over 180, they were first astounded, then humbled, then dedicated to meeting his overwhelming intellectual needs.

After meeting with staff at Tokyo University, ten-year old Oshiba was admitted to the engineering department and awarded a high honor: he was given an all-paid scholarship to the University. The professor of the Engineering Department, Tadatomo Suga, was so impressed with Billy he enabled the young genius to live in an apartment on the craggy hilltop "Dungeon" known as Asano Campus.

Oshiba adapted to university life immediately; his intellectual curiosity overwhelmed the ache he felt being separated from his parents. Because he scored at the top in all subjects, he flourished not only in engineering, but in precision engineering and the fracture mechanics characterization of metal-ceramics, a little-known subject he quickly learned from Suga, quickly becoming an expert in that field.

Other subjects the campus offered that Oshiba devoured were Cryogenic Research, astronomy, physics and mathematics, and he became a member of JIEP, the Japan Institute of Electronics. But his real love: computers.

He saw a vast potential in this new, fledgling industry with its algorithms and microchips and soon was spending most of his time in the computer lab. He also studied English and became proficient by the time he was fourteen.

Meanwhile, his father was offered a job with G.M. in the United States and moved there when Billy was twelve. After graduating with top honors from the University and holding numerous degrees, he was offered a top position at Fujitsu where his reputation exploded, leading to the offer from Vincent Fazio to do private work for him.

....

It had been a harrowing two days for the young genius. The day before had seen the initiation of Fazio's campaign against the American military complex.

Due to the glitch that had caused the trucks to speed resulting in the accident and consequent notoriety of the two behemoths, Oshiba had received a scorching call from Vincent excoriating him for the error. Billy had spoken with his mechanical crew and given them directions for the cure, which they'd performed, but Fazio had insisted he come and check the trucks himself at the designated rendezvous at the farm house in New Mexico.

Billy had left Fazio's truck manufacturing facility around noon in one of his Jags and made it to the farm house a little before Fazio and J.J. had arrived with the Phoenix cop who was tracking the trucks. Then there was the incident with the mechanic who'd disobeyed protocol and gotten himself torn to bits by the Jolly Green Giant. Oshiba had gotten little sleep and now he was stuck in traffic on I-70 for God knows why … on top of it all, he was hungry and had to relieve himself; he couldn't wait much longer.

Traffic was clogged for miles at this checkpoint set up with barriers to stop any suspicious vehicles, but Oshiba wasn't aware of the recent developments.

Troopers were stopping traffic on the east-bound route, feeding cars from the three lane highway to the right lane only.

The black Jaguar moved up to a police officer at the checkpoint.

"May I see your license?" the officer asked.

"Sure," the young Asian man answered, handing the officer his license.

The officer studied the license, looked at the Asian, then back to the license, then called another officer over and showed him the license.

"Please step out of your car."

"Is anything wrong, officer?" Billy Oshiba said as he exited the car and was immediately surrounded by a squad of police.

....

Exxon Service Station On 1-20 Near Louisiana
4:30 p.m. Central Time

The information Manny had gained from the map taken off the dead terrorist at the truck stop had been priceless. The authorities had quickly developed a plan to intercept the trucks at the next refueling stop which was at an Exxon Station on 1-20 near Louisiana.

Three FBI agents disguised as construction workers had the exit blocked off.

Inside the station, Manny and Joey were waiting along with half a dozen agents and troopers. All were wearing masks. Several bullet-ridden cars, a pick-up truck, and an eighteen wheeler, along with their "dead" motorists, had been carefully staged by federal authorities.

Behind the station, hidden from view, Fazio's black van, which had been captured by the FBI, was parked near an FBI chopper. Sharon was at the controls. Inside the black van, two FBI agents were guarding the bound captives, who were sitting on the floor blindfolded.

The two trucks slowed as they approached the exit ramp. Baldwin, along with Special Agents Moufti and Stoner, were disguised as construction workers. They spoke in whispers.

"Why don't we just blow these fuckers away?" Agent Moufti said.

"Because of the chemical weapons. We've got to get a man inside to knock out the computers," Baldwin said.

The three agents removed the barriers allowing the trucks to enter the off ramp.

"Alert: They're on their way in, " Baldwin said into his walkie talkie.

At the station, Manny answered "Roger," and nodded to Joey.

As the trucks pulled in, the men, including Manny, moved to the lead truck.

Inside the truck, the radar system was scanning the scene outside. A TV monitor showed images of the hooded men and riddled cars.

Outside the lead truck, Manny was nearing the fuel tank when he looked across the station and saw a young boy riding his bicycle across the desert toward the station. When the boy arrived, he went to an air pump and pumped air in his tires.

Breen felt an uneasiness about the boy; he couldn't anticipate what was going to happen once he entered the truck. Having another element to deal with, this child, could be a problem.

Manny hesitated, then decided to proceed with the plan. He retrieved the gold key from his belt and inserted it into the panel near the truck's fuel tank. He lifted the panel revealing the blinking lights and digital keyboard. Breen didn't notice that the boy was on his bike and riding toward the rear truck.

Manny finished punching in the access code. He was about to grab the fuel cap (omitting to input the password which would have resulted in his death) when he looked up and saw the boy approaching the rear truck.

"Damn!" Manny said, swearing under his breath. Pausing in the operation, he saw the curious kid stop, get off his bike, and walk toward the truck. Knowing of the truck's lethal defensive devices when approached without proper protection, Manny ran toward the boy and shouted, "NO! STAY AWAY!"

Inside the truck, the boy's snooping had activated the truck's warning system screen which popped on instantly picturing a diagram of the rear truck. A red light began flashing rapidly at the spot the boy was approaching; the warning began flashing:

UNAUTHORIZED ENCROACHMENT

Manny dove at the boy, knocking him to the ground just as the truck's defensive measure activated a machine-gun burst that fired over their heads. The words

"ABORT! ABORT!"

appeared on the computer screen of the rear truck.

Inside the lead truck, gears shifted automatically.

The trucks began moving away as the lead truck maneuvered broadside to the FBI agents. A panel slid up revealing the missile rack.

Manny grabbed the boy, ran to a ditch on the other side of the station, and dove into it with Joey right behind as the truck fired a missile: it hit the pumps causing a massive explosion killing most of the agents.

Inside the malignant monsters, the computer screens were swiftly adjusting to the changed plan as the words appeared:

CONVERTING TO AUXILIARY TANKS -
ACTIVATE MOBILE REFUELING SEQUENCE

This was followed by a series of quickly running numbers spitting out letter/number combinations.

At the exit off I-20, Baldwin, Moufti, and Stoner saw the explosion.

"SHIT!" Baldwin shouted as he drew his .45 and sprinted for the station with the other two agents close behind.

. . . .

A gasoline tanker truck a short distance west of the Exxon station was parked on the shoulder. Inside the tanker, the driver turned off a blinking red button, pulled into the slow lane, and began picking up speed.

. . . .

At the Exxon station, Manny watched as the two trucks pulled out and headed for the access road leading to I-20 East. Breen quickly checked the boy. "You okay?"

The bewildered boy shook his head. "Yeah, I think so …"

Manny tousled the kid's hair and ran to an all-purpose-terrain-vehicle parked beside the service station with the engine running. The FBI had prepared it for just such an emergency. Breen grabbed an automatic weapon lying on the ground, hopped into the vehicle, and jammed it into gear. Joey ran up and jumped in as Manny took off.

Behind the burning station, Baldwin and two other agents hightailed it around the building, ran to the chopper where Sharon was waiting, and got aboard.

"Let's go!" Baldwin shouted as the chopper lifted off.

....

On I-20 East, the trucks entered, moved to the fast lane and quickly picked up speed as the chopper sliced through the air keeping a discreet distance behind the trucks.

Manny and Joey were speeding across the flat desert in the terrain vehicle to the right of and paralleling the trucks. They saw the gasoline tanker pass the rear truck which slowed, allowing the tanker to move between it and the lead truck. A nozzle protruded from the tanker; it began refueling the lead truck much as a jet is refueled in mid-air.

In the terrain vehicle, Manny shouted to Joey: "YOUR INSURANCE PAID UP?"

"WHAT INSURANCE?" Joey shouted back as Manny swerved over toward the highway.

A computer screen in the rear truck was furiously computing the situation as the following data appeared:

"DANGER: HOLD FIRE - REFUELING

PROCESS IN PROGRESS"

The word DANGER was flashing.

The two trucks and the tanker were tearing down the highway in the fast lane single file as Manny and Joey knifed onto the middle lane from the shoulder and sped up, paralleling the refueling tanker. Manny honked his horn at the driver of the tanker, who ignored Manny and continued the refueling process.

"GO FOR THE TIRES!" Manny shouted to Joey.

"YOU HAVE TO TELL ME TO GO FOR THE TIRES? I KNOW TO GO FOR THE TIRES! DO I TELL YOU HOW TO DRIVE?"

"ALL THE TIME!"

"I'LL GO FOR THE TIRES!"

Joey fired a blast from his automatic weapon at the driver-driven tanker's tires causing the tires to explode on impact. The tanker wobbled, then careened onto the left shoulder as the driver struggled to regain control.

In the chopper, Sharon and Baldwin saw what was happening on the road below and realized they were in imminent danger if there was a gasoline explosion.

"LOOK OUT!" Baldwin shouted, but Sharon, being a combat hardened veteran, had already flared the chopper to the left away from the highway.

In a sudden violent move, the tanker slowed, jackknifed, skidded off the shoulder, overturned, and exploded.

Manny swerved to avoid the tremendous impact as the tanker fragmented and a red fireball shot into the sky, just missing the chopper.

The rear truck took an off-ramp as the lead truck continued east on I-20. Inside, the computer screen's danger light was flashing on the words:

AUXILIARY FUEL TANK MALFUNCTION

FUEL LEVEL CRITICAL

REPAIR IN PROGRESS

Manny and Joey followed behind the second truck, keeping a quarter mile space behind it to avoid activating the trucks' defensive mechanisms.

The chopper was above, traveling with them at the same speed.

A sign reading KILGORE TEXAS, 10 MILES, loomed up ahead.

....

As it entered a residential street in Kilgore, the lone sister truck slowed and came to a stop beside a vacant baseball field, engine idling.

Four blocks behind, Manny and Joey pulled over and stopped next to a vacant lot as Sharon brought the chopper down in the lot. Manny and Joey ran to the chopper as Baldwin and the two agents emerged holding gas masks.

Manny pointed. "It's about four blocks down. What about the other truck?"

"I've got a team keeping track of that baby," Baldwin said.

Baldwin handed extra gas masks to Manny and Joey. "It's a good thing you didn't open that fuel tank. There's a password that has to be inputted after the access code … without that, you're history," Agent Baldwin said. "They picked up a guy named Oshiba. Said he programmed the trucks. He was bragging about it."

As they talked, they walked toward the truck. Manny checked the magazine of his automatic weapon. "What's the password?"

"Oshiba wouldn't talk, but he gave us a clue. He said it's the most-used seven letter word in New York City."

Manny smiled. "That's easy. I had a couple of buddies in the Marine Corp. from Brooklyn."

The team split up. Manny approached from the right side, Joey and the agents from the left. As he neared the rear of the truck, Manny took the protective badge he'd removed from one of the men at the warehouse and pinned it to his shirt, then retrieved the gold key from his belt and stuck it in his pocket.

As Joey and the FBI agents moved in cautiously from the other side, Breen reached the truck and stepped over to the panel. He slipped the key into the lock, pushed a button that said "REAR ENTRANCE," punched in the access number, then paused.

"The password has to be …" he said to himself as he pulled the gold key from his pocket … Manny typed in the word:

"ASSHOLE"

… which was a good guess. The truck's back panel slid open.

As Joey, Baldwin, and the other agents stopped fifty feet from the truck and snapped on their gas masks, Baldwin's walkie talkie beeped. It was Sharon yelling: "WATCH OUT! THE OTHER TRUCK IS COMING AT YOU RIGHT NOW! IT'S SIX BLOCKS AWAY!"

"EVERYBODY DOWN!" Baldwin shouted. The men hit the ground as the second truck suddenly barreled around the corner and headed straight for its sister.

Inside the parked sister truck, the computer screen registered the flashing command:

"AUXILIARY FUEL TANK REPAIRED"

Immediately the rear panel started to close as the gears in the truck shifted automatically and the truck began to move.

Manny, who'd been about to enter the rear of the truck, saw it moving away, made a snap decision, ran up to it and dove inside just as the panel door slammed shut behind him.

Inside the moving vehicle, Manny put his gas mask on … then realized he was trapped in a narrow, confined space.

"Not too bright, Manny," he yelled frantically, "NOT TOO BRIGHT!" He began pounding on the rear panel door. It didn't budge. Breen whirled around facing the interior of the truck, eyes wide with fear. His point of view through the gas mask was distorted, fuzzy, as a red light began blinking over the panel marked Last Resort and the panel slid up. Manny had lost his protective badge.

The Jolly Green Giant, the huge faceless robot, stood recessed in the wall. Its eyes began to glow as it activated with a hum, then stepped out of the enclosure and slowly, methodically, surveyed the truck's interior.

Manny saw the robot emerge through the distortion of his gas mask, just as a whitish, poisonous mist began to permeate the interior, obscuring the robot's location.

The lethal mist was growing more dense as Manny struggled to see through it …

Breen had lost track of the robot. A sudden intuition spun him around as the mechanical killer loomed up behind him. It reached for Manny just as he ducked and moved away, disappearing in the swirling muck.

The robot's eyes slowly scanned the interior searching the gloom with infrared night vision as Manny crouched behind the bank of computers. The robot bent down, scanned the floor, located the legs of his prey, and moved off to the attack.

As the robot moved up behind him, Manny sensed his approach, dropped to the floor and rolled away just as the metal machine slammed its fist at the place where Manny's head had been, knocking down a computer terminal.

Breen jumped to his feet and fired a sustained blast at the robot as it struck out at Manny with a backhanded slap that knocked the cop from Phoenix against the side of the truck. As Breen slid down with his back to the wall, stunned, he saw the robot's crotch as the robot closed in for the kill.

What looked like a huge cod piece covered its groin area giving it the appearance of having male organs.

"A robot with balls?" Manny said as he fired a blast at the cod piece and rolled away at the last instant as the robot tried to stomp him to death.

Manny was now behind the monster. "Over here, dickhead!" Manny shouted. The robot whirled around as Manny fired again at his crotch. Bullets bounced off, but the cod piece started to loosen.

The robot stalked Manny swinging at him repeatedly as Manny backed up and dodged getting off a few more rounds at the robot's privates.

"What do they call you, Robostud?"

The robot's cod piece was dangling now revealing the myriad blinking lights and wires in the robot's central command panel. As Breen was about to fire again, he tripped and fell, losing his automatic weapon.

The robot clanked toward the prone figure as Manny looked up and saw it towering over him. The hunk of metal raised its arms to crush him as Manny retrieved his weapon from the floor and fired a final blast at the robot's crotch, shattering it and destroying its power source. The robot shuddered as smoke emerged from its privates. Its eyes crossed, it stumbled backwards, and then collapsed onto the computers.

Manny jumped up as the computers short circuited. Smoke added to the grey mist filling the truck's interior, and as Manny stepped by the dying robot, one of its thrashing claws loosened his gas mask.

Manny took a deep, deep breath as the mask fell off. This was a time when his breath-holding skill was vital. Manny shot into the remaining computers, dealing the truck the coup de grace. On one of the dying screens, Breen saw the truck's final destination:

PENNSYLVANIA AVENUE, WASHINGTON, D.C.

Outside, the truck wandered off the road into a field where it moved slowly in circles as it died. The back panel was still closed.

Inside, Manny's air supply was exhausted. He emptied his automatic weapon into the last remaining computer terminal causing the rear door to slide up.

Breen dove out of the truck and rolled away from the deadly fumes until he was at a safe distance. He sat up gulping fresh air, then watched as the last of the smoking truck's power short-circuited and snatches of Mr. Rogers' singing died away.

....

On a winding road several miles away, the lead truck sat overlooking the valley where its sister truck had been destroyed. Inside the truck, the computer screen began flashing:

PROCEED ALONE TO DESTINATION

....

In the valley below, Longbow Apaches and a CH47 Chinook had landed near Manny. Soldiers, wearing Nuclear, Biological and Chemical gear poured out of the Chinook and surrounded the truck. Joey, Baldwin and Sharon ran over to Manny.

"You okay?" Sharon asked with concern.

"I'm okay, Sharon, the adrenalin's still pumping, but I'm okay."

As they headed for the chopper, Baldwin brought him up to date: "We've got a briefing with the Joint Chiefs in D.C. in six hours, that's …" Baldwin looked at his watch … " … that's two a.m. They've got a C20B at Lackland ready and waiting."

Manny stopped, shook his head. "I can't do that, I can't be confined like that. Joey, Sharon, tell him."

"Look, buddy," Joey said, his voice strong, "it's national security, you got to suck it up, get past your problem …"

"Yeah? What if I told you you got to stop rooting for the Giants? You think you could do that without a problem?"

"That's not fair!"

"Yeah, but it's life, pal."

"Okay, okay," Joey said, "tell you what. I'll give up the Giants if you get on that plane."

Manny looked at him. "You would do that? Really?"

"Yeah, really, my word." Joey held up his hand.

"Okay, I'll give it a try. But I catch you watchin' a game, you have to pay me a week's salary."

"Deal. You're in the Apache."

"It's a two-seater, Manny," Sharon said, "you can sit by the door and keep it open, just like in the Notar!"

Manny smiled and climbed in the Longbow.

Joey, Baldwin and Sharon entered the Sikorski. The choppers lifted off, leaving the mop-up and gathering of evidence to the ground troops.

……….

Third Day

Andrews Air Force Base in Washington, D.C.
2:00 a.m. Eastern Time

The C20B jet was sitting on the runway as a groggy Manny Breen exited the jet. Joey was behind him, followed by Baldwin and Sharon.

"Think he's going to be okay? He's been through a lot," Baldwin said to Sharon as they walked toward the hangar.

"When the effect wears off," Sharon replied. "At Lackland, I gave him enough sleeping pills to knock out a rhino. It was the only way he'd get on the plane."

....

Tank Room Of The Pentagon In Arlington County, Virginia
2:20 a.m. Eastern Time

A limo pulled up to one of the security gates, a guard stopped the car, the driver flashed his I.D., the guard waved the limo in.

The Pentagon, the headquarters of The Department of Defense as well as the National Military Command Center, was composed of five concentric pentagonal buildings with five stories each that were located both in the Commonwealth of Virginia and in Washington, D.C. This anomaly was explained by the fact that the dividing line between D.C. and Virginia was down the center of the Potomac River, and a section of the Pentagon rested on land dredged from the river.

The "E Ring" and the "A Ring" referred to names given to the outermost section and the innermost section of the five-sided building, the outermost section having the highest priority. The Tank Room was located in the "A Ring."

A long dark table split the windowless Tank Room in half. Ordinarily it seated twelve individuals in brown leather chairs, but to accommodate the extra personnel for this special early a.m. session, two chairs had been added, bringing the total to fourteen. Nearby was an additional table seating another five entities. As usual, on the table in front of each chair were a pad, pencil and small bowl of candy.

Paintings were carefully placed on the walls, and at one end of the room there were seven flags, including the American flag and the flags of the military services. At the other end there was an opaque screen for projecting slides and films.

The usual protocol for the Pentagon meetings was for the ops deps (the operations deputies) to first check issues that were to be passed to the Joint Chiefs before they could be scrutinized by the Chairman and his staff, but because of the present urgent crisis facing the nation, a special meeting had been called for two a.m. circumventing the protocol.

Already seated were the Joint Chiefs Chairman and the heads of the four military branches, White House Advisor Bruce Carrouthers, FBI Chief Warner Bullock, CIA Director Phil Conklin and Senator Sam Jackman, Chairman of the Select Committee on Intelligence.

A furious Jackman faced FBI Chief Bullock as Manny and Baldwin entered and sat at the table.

"Super trucks? For God's sake, Bullock, how do you explain this? Where's the FBI been?"

The Joint Chiefs Chairman, Admiral Royce Sayles, tall and hawk-nosed, was seated beside Bullock. A blunt-speaking Scots Irishman, he shared

Jackman's anger. "Yeah, everybody's sitting around with his finger up his ass —!"

"I'm not going to be the fucking scapegoat here!" Bullock shouted, his face turning crimson.

Presidential Advisor Carrouthers addressed Jackman. "Senator, the President's concern is for the American people, he …"

"The President's concern is for his own ass!" Jackmana said, spitting out his reply. "If he was so concerned, where the hell is he? On a golfing trip to Florida? He never shows up during a crisis! Jesus, what a wimp!"

"Senator, I resent —-"

"HOLD IT!" Admiral Sayles yelled, "Everybody just calm down!"

Senator Jackman looked around the table. "Can anybody explain how these trucks even exist?"

Agent Baldwin stood up. "I'm Special Agent Don Baldwin. We've been following the trucks, we think we know who built 'em, but first, Det. Breen of the Phoenix Police Department will fill you in on their design …"

"A detective?" Bullock shouted. "What's a detective doing here? This is a national security crisis, for Christ's sake!"

"He has first-hand knowledge of the trucks …" Baldwin began. Bullock cut him off.

"——I don't give a holy fuck if he built the damn things, he doesn't have clearance!"

Manny stuck his finger in the air. "Clear this, numb nuts!"

Bullock's face was ashen. "You can't talk ——"

"SHUT UP, BULLOCK!" Admiral Sayles yelled, then to Manny: "Go ahead, Det. Breen."

An Army Lieutenant wheeled in a stand showing a diagram of the trucks. Manny approached it, pointing to specific areas as he spoke.

"I had this diagram drawn up because I was inside one of the trucks. They were programmed to carry out a precise military operation, one protecting the other like a battleship protecting a carrier. Their destination: Blow up the White House!

"The rear truck, now inoperable, carried a Chinese MLRS, multiple launch rocket system with 19 tubes. What makes the remaining truck so dangerous? It carries a chemical agent, probably some kind of botulism."

"Jesus!" the Senator said, "and the explanation for how all this is possible?"

"The man who built the trucks is Vincent Fazio," Baldwin said, he's a billionaire, manufactures trucks and has a DOD contract to make the M1 Tank. He also has top security clearance. His son was killed by friendly fire in the Gulf War."

Senator Jackman nodded. "I remember him. He told the President to fuck off."

"That's him," Manny said. "He's ex-CIA. We think one of his buddies may have used CIA satellites to program the trucks' terrain maps."

Phil Conklin, CIA Chief, spoke out. "Vincent Fazio is one of our best field agents, I can't believe he'd turn on his own country and do something so horrific!"

"We have proof it's him," Manny said, "he tried to have me killed."

Admiral Sayles said, "So you say the trucks are totally computerized? No drivers?"

"That's right."

"Son-of-a-bitch!" Admiral Sayles said, then to Conklin: "Any idea who might have access to those satellites?"

"The only man who could do it is John Jamington Fryer, head of Counterintelligence."

"Get him over here," Sayles demanded.

Conklin shook his head. "He's in Europe on an assignment."

"I don't think so. I think he's the man I saw with Fazio," Manny said.

Senator Jackman scanned the room. "Alright, gentlemen, our next move?"

"We've already turned the White House into an armed camp," Rear Admiral Petrie said, "so it's secure."

Admiral Sayles nodded. "Okay. Now we have to find a way to stop that second truck without blowing up half the country."

"I know how," Manny said. The room was silent as everyone looked at the Phoenix cop.

. . . .

I-40 Eastbound Ten Miles East of Crossville,
Tennessee
6:30 a.m. Central Time

The surviving truck was speeding through the early morning light on a deserted highway.

....

A mile back on I-40, a Plymouth was following the lethal machine with three CIA agents inside keeping the truck under surveillance. Farther back, two Longbow Apaches were following. Inside the Apaches, the truck was illuminated on their fire control system and their powerful AN/AWG-9 radars were spitting out high-frequency signals.

As the early morning sun peeked over the horizon, the lone devastator picked up speed and headed directly into the blinding rays of brilliance toward D.C.

At an entrance ramp ahead of the truck, several "ordinary" cars were waiting for the truck to approach. Baldwin, waiting in the lead car with several other agents, spoke into the radio: "All units, all units, remember, our objective is only to observe. Do not engage the truck, do not engage the truck!"

At another entrance ahead, more cars were waiting filled with FBI agents as Baldwin's warning was received: "Do not, repeat, do not, engage the truck …".

The radio was filled with loud static as the truck's electronic jamming system kicked in.

……….

The highway below was straight as I-40 began to climb steadily from 1800 feet at Crossville toward the Cumberland Plateau. Further east, the highway entered the Crab Orchard Mountains and here, the highway dropped over two hundred feet and came to a narrow valley. Ahead, the Interstate would be entering the Eastern Time Zone, but the narrow valley near Crab Orchard Gap was the target for the Huey Army Chopper speeding south, the strategic coordinate where the chopper was going to intercept the truck speeding east.

Behind the Huey on either side were two Hueys riding shotgun.

Inside the lead chopper, Sharon was at the controls. Manny was sitting beside her making calculations on a mini-calculator from a map he was holding on his knees. The chopper door beside him was open.

"Thanks for going to bat for me to fly this mission, Manny," Sharon said, "you know I appreciate this opportunity to serve my country."

Manny replied without looking up. "With your combat background in the Gulf War and first-hand experience with the trucks, you were the obvious choice."

A voice came over the chopper radio: "Able Charley 10, Able Charley 10, this is Hector 5 ..."

Well behind the Hueys skimming low over 1-10 were four Longbow Apaches. Inside the lead chopper the pilot was checking his instruments as his co-pilot studied the terrain below.

"Do you read?" The pilot said. Sharon's voice came through with clarity: "Roger, go ahead, Hector Five."

The pilot continued: "Feeding in land speed coordinates: Target traveling at 61 knots and holding steady ..." he checked his instrument panel ... " ... wind velocity, 5.2 knots south southeast ... target is now 8.3 kilometers from point of intercept which I place at 0600 hours."

Inside the Huey, Manny was inputting the co-ordinates with a slide rule, drawing two intersecting lines on the map that met at a point on I-40 over the narrow valley.

Below and one mile ahead, the lone Super Truck was speeding toward the entrance ramp where the FBI/CIA agents were waiting. As it passed the ramp, the agents' cars entered I-40, falling in a half mile behind as the early morning sun peeked over the horizon.

As they flew over the Obed River, Manny fin-ished checking his watch, leaned out of the door and looked down at the shadow of the Huey moving along the ground. What he saw was a long cable extended from the aircraft; at the bottom of the cable was a huge, iron wrecking ball … anyone seeing the Huey from the ground might have been reminded of the opening scene in La Dolce Vita in which a helicopter was carrying a statue of Jesus, dangling from a cable, to the Vatican.

The Huey was skimming over a mountainous area bordering I-40 on one side and a steep drop-off on the other side toward I-40 and Lake Tansi. The hills were keeping the surviving truck from picking up the chopper on its radar as the two continued on a converging path, the truck heading due east, the chopper due south.

Sharon's chopper was flying low through a narrow pass approaching the highway at a right angle as the Super Truck approached the spot where it would intersect briefly with the narrow pass.

Inside the truck, one of its computers was ticking off numbers at an incredible rate as the distance to D.C. on the computer screen read 782 miles.

Inside the Huey, Manny, perspiring heavily, made a final check of his coordinates. "Hold it steady, Sharon."

Sharon nodded. "Steady as she goes …" She glanced at her co-pilot. "You okay?"

"I can breathe, I'm okay," he said, repeating the mantra. Sharon smiled.

The Huey churned low through the pass, nose down. Ahead, the valley with the narrow section of I-40 suddenly popped into view.

On I-40, the truck was speeding toward the same narrow section where the chopper was going to intercept.

There was an instant of heart-stopping anticipation, then the truck barreled into the intersect point, the Huey zoomed up out of the pass like an avenging harpy and caught the truck off guard. Before the super beast's computers had time to react, the Huey shot low over it, but the wrecking ball barely scraped the truck's roof.

Manny looked back at the unscathed truck. "What happened?"

"We hit an updraft, didn't figure —-!"

East of the chopper on I-40, the truck's missile rack panel slid up.

Inside the Huey, Sharon quickly flipped switches, activating the aircraft's new defense system against missiles, both surface-to-air and air-to-air. A series of flares and balloons ejected from the tail section as the two missiles fired from the truck homed in on the decoys and exploded.

"The wrecking ball limits our maneuverability," Sharon said as she dropped the chopper lower.

"Go around those hills," Manny said, "we have to keep the truck distracted; it's within range of D.C."

The Huey curved around speeding due east and knifed over a series of hills, reached I-40 ahead of the truck and turned back west on a collision course.

The chopper swept toward the truck as the truck began spitting machine gun fire from a mount just above the hood.

As they met, the wrecking ball smashed into the top of the truck demolishing the black dome as the truck fired another missile at the receding chopper. The missile, deflected by the Huey's infrared countermeasure system and decoy flares, slammed into a hill behind the chopper as the helicopter knifed sharply to the right.

"There's another pass up ahead, it's our last chance," Manny said.

Sharon nodded. "We'll make this one count!"

The Huey entered a mountain pass, curved sharply around, and headed back south toward the highway as the cable holding the wrecking ball began to unravel.

The truck was approaching the pass ahead with all its weapon systems visible, bared for a final confrontation.

Sharon brought the chopper in low over the hilly area as the cable holding the wrecking ball unraveled further ...

Arriving suddenly at the I-40 East coordinate, the Huey zoomed up and out of the pass at top speed just as the truck shot into view.

The timing was perfect. The wrecking ball connected with the upper portion of the Super Truck's body with a terrifying crash, knocking the monster off the highway as the wrecking ball came loose and fell down the steep drop with the truck.

The chopper executed a sharp turn bringing the Huey back over the truck as Sharon and Manny looked down and saw the battered hunk of metal roll over, then tumble down the ravine.

"Great flying, Sharon, you should get a medal!" Manny said, giving his pilot the high-five.

"I'll settle for a beer and a chili dog," Sharon responded with a laugh.

The Huey curved away ... as the van with the words

"A MOVING EXPERIENCE!"

painted on the sides passed underneath on the highway and sped east undetected.

....

FBI Headquarters in Washington, D.C.
3:00 p.m. Eastern Time

Manny, Baldwin and crew, including Sharon and FBI Director Bullock, were seated in a conference room.

Manny was exhausted. He'd been going non-stop for over forty-eight hours and looked it.

"Oshiba told us everything we need to know to arrest and charge Vincent Fazio and John Jamington Fryer," Baldwin said. "Now all we have to do is find them."

Director Bullock was holding one of the flyers dispersed by the clown at the White House two days earlier. "What about this?"

Baldwin took the flyer, examined it, and tossed it on the table as the phone rang.

"Yeah?" Bullock answered, then, "Hold on." He gave Manny the phone. "It's for you."

"Breen," Manny said into the receiver.

"Manny, it's Ho," the voice said, "I have some info regarding Vince, Jr's death, I think it could be important."

"Go ahead, Charlie."

"I called Mrs. Fazio, Vincent Junior's mother," Ho began, "I asked her when her son was born. You ready? She said it was August 21, 1971."

"August 21st?" Manny said. "That's today."

"That's right," Ho replied. "Today's the 21st.! We watched the tape of Fazio at the cemetery. He said he was going to the White House, but not to get a piece of metal. And you know the specific time of birth? Three fifteen p.m."

"Thanks, Charlie," Manny said as he hung up, crossed to the table, picked up the flyer and read it out loud. "Celebration: August 21, 3:15." Manny looked at his watch. "Five after three." He flashed on the moving van with the words "A MOVING EX-PERIENCE!" written on the side at the truck stop and remembered what Fazio had said at the farm-house about "A moving experience ..." Suddenly it all came together.

"Holy ——! There's a third truck! THERE'S A THIRD TRUCK! He's going to hit the White House in ten minutes!" The door slammed shut behind Manny's back.

"BREEN!" Baldwin yelled, but the Phoenix cop was gone.

....

Pennsylvania Avenue NW in Washington, D.C.
3:05 p.m. Eastern Time

Pennsylvania Avenue NW ran for over five miles inside D.C., but the mile from the White House to the United States Capitol was the most vital and heavily traveled section.

In 1993, all vehicular traffic was allowed on this two-way asphalt constructed roadway as well as sightseers, always plentiful in the summer, who came for a chance to get a glimpse of the President and soak up history.

Manny shot out of the FBI building and sprinted west on the north side of the Avenue. The White House was six blocks away.

It was a hot August day in the Capitol. The sun was scorching from a cloudless sky as Manny, already perspiring, ran at top speed, dodging between gawking pedestrians including families with children. In under a minute, he'd reached 15th Street NW, one block from the White House with the Treasury Building on his left.

And there it was! He was right. The black domed moving van with the words

"A MOVING EXPERIENCE!"

printed on the sides was parked on 15th ST. NW at the intersection of 15th and Pennsylvania, heading toward the Avenue. Several men were sitting in a parked car behind the van.

Manny recognized Vincent Fazio and J.J. standing in the street beside the parked car, a Lexus SC, speaking with the two men inside. Fazio, who was carrying a large shopping bag, was looking toward the East Wing of the White House.

Breen, careful to stay incognito behind a crowd of tourists, reached 15th Street NW and slowed as Fazio and J.J. left the two men, walked behind their parked car and entered their BMW parked a few feet away. As Breen approached, the moving van turned the corner and slowly headed west on Pennsylvania Avenue toward the White House one block away, followed by the two cars.

A reception was being held on the lawn for foreign dignitaries; the President was due to arrive momentarily. Manny could hear music blaring on the White House lawn.

Breen, staying behind the group, was still on the north side of Pennsylvania Avenue, following the caravan slowly moving west toward the White House.

....

A Bell AH-1W Super Cobra lifted off the chopper pad at FBI Headquarters and moved low over Pennsylvania Avenue with Sharon piloting. Baldwin was inside with other FBI agents.

The Super Cobra was a powerful twin-engine attack chopper, superbly fitted for the coming fire-fight. It's features? A three barrel 20mm Xm197 cannon based on the six barrel M61 Vulcan cannon. It had a modified fire control system designed to carry and fire AIM Sidewinder and AGM-114 Hellfire Missiles as well as multiple machine gun mounts.

....

The moving van slowed when it was directly opposite the White House and stopped in the middle of the street. The driver stuck his head out the window and looked back at a flat tire on the van. Police cars were parked on the south side of Pennsylvania Avenue in front of the iron fence.

A crowd was standing on the wide sidewalk in front of the fence watching the proceedings on the White House lawn.

A motorcycle cop patrolling the area approached the driver of the moving van.

"You can't stop here," the cop said, sitting on his motorcycle with the engine idling.

"I've got a flat," the driver said with a big smile.

The cop removed his dark glasses. "You'll have to fix it somewhere else, you can't stop here."

Fazio and J.J. stopped beside the van, got out of their BMW and approached the cop in the street. "These are my things he's moving, officer," Fazio said, still carrying the shopping bag. "Sorry this happened. We'll move it off ..."

The van started to move, but the cop, who'd been looking at the Arizona license plates, got off the motorcycle. "Hold it. Open it up," he said to Fazio.

Fazio feigned innocence. "Anything wrong, officer?," Fazio said, taking a fountain pen out of his suit jacket.

The cop was more insistent this time. His hand was on his gun. "Just open it. Now!"

"Certainly."

Fazio walked with the officer to the rear of the van where the BMW was parked, took out a key and then 'accidentally' dropped the pen on the cement.

"My Silver Cross Pen," Fazio said, smiling, "don't want to lose that!"

He bent over to pick it up as the officer noticed the shopping bag. "What's in the bag?"

"Hand grenades." Fazio stood up and fired a silent bullet from the 'pen' into the cop's head, killing him instantly.

The two men got out of the Lexus and pulled the dead cop inside. They were closing the door when Manny approached on the sidewalk with a big smile. He'd observed the officer's assassination.

"Hi, Vince, it's me, the lowbrow cop from Phoenix … nice pen!"

Fazio's eyes widened. "Kill the son-of-a-bitch!"

The two men fired repeatedly at Breen who instantly ducked behind a series of parked cars unharmed.

The van's rear panel slid up; twelve men, the Fazio Squad (FS), sprang out, armed with M27s, Pigs (M60s) and AMPADS (surface-to-air missiles) wearing body armor;

Simultaneously, a ramp slid out of the truck with an ominous hum, a 155mm truck-mounted Howitzer rolled down the ramp onto the street, then took up a position with the cannon pointed toward the White House as the FS deployed in a protective semi-circle in front of the Howitzer;

At the sound of gunfire, police officers who'd been talking to tourists at the iron gate drew their Glocks and ducked for cover behind their squad cars;

Snipers appeared on the roof of the White House;

Secret Service hurried everyone off the lawn as an Agent grabbed the bull horn: "EVERYONE TAKE COVER! TAKE COVER! MOVE AWAY FROM THE WHITE HOUSE, I REPEAT, MOVE AWAY FROM THE WHITE HOUSE!!"

....

Manny was crouched on the sidewalk behind a parked car. Fazio pulled a grenade from his shopping bag and tossed it over the top of the BMW at the cops, killing four and blowing up two of their squad cars. He and J.J. jumped back in their car, J.J. jammed on the ignition, made a sharp U-turn, and headed back east on Pennsylvania Avenue, away from Breen toward 15th Street.

An Abrams M-1 Tank turned the corner from 15th Street onto Pennsylvania a block away headed directly at the BMW.

J.J. slammed on the brakes, backed up, tires squealing, made another quick U-turn, and started back in the opposite direction going west on the Avenue, again speeding past Manny who was still on the sidewalk behind the van.

The Howitzer on the Caesar swiveled right and blasted the Sherman on 15th Street as a second tank turned the corner at 17th and Pennsylvania in the opposite direction heading east coming directly at the BMW.

J.J. cut over to the wide sidewalk on the White House side of the Avenue headed toward 17th Street. As the BMW neared the tank, the cannon on the Caesar swiveled left and fired a round obliterating the second Sherman.

Partially caught in the blast, the BMW swerved violently, careened out of control, and smashed into a tree on Pennsylvania near The Ellipse. Fazio and J.J. sat in the car stunned as the Howitzer poured another round into a third tank behind its burning sister on 17th.

. . . .

The Howitzer had a two man crew that fired anti-tank Fragmentation Bomblets and guided anti-tank munitions. Its 12mm machine gun was already tearing law enforcement personnel on the street to shreds as well as decimating snipers on the White House roof.

The barrel of the Howitzer swiveled toward the police cars lined up on the south side of the Avenue facing the White House, fired another projectile and demolished six squad cars throwing policemen in the air like a dry dandelion finger-thunked. Simultaneously, a half dozen police cars speeding east on Pennsylvania Avenue from 17th Street were blown into the air with a fifth and sixth anti-tank projectile.

. . . .

Breen, still crouched behind the parked car on Pennsylvania, identified the Caesar instantly and knew it had a six round capacity with sixty seconds to reload. He had to act quickly. And he had to arm himself.

Manny's first objective: eliminate Fazio's Squad and the machine gun mounted on the Caesar.

He looked around to familiarize himself with the terrain and saw a man and woman with a small child huddled on the sidewalk beside a parked car on the north side of the Avenue twenty yards away near 15th St. First, he had to secure their safety. Staying low, protected by the parked cars, he ran to the family.

"IS THIS YOUR CAR?" Manny shouted over the gunfire.

"YES," the man answered.

"GET IN AND STAY LOW!" It was a young husband and wife with a five-year old child. The boy was wearing a cowboy suit complete with hat and boots with two cap guns stuck in his holsters.

Manny had an idea. "LET ME BORROW YOUR GUNS! I'LL GIVE 'EM BACK, I PROMISE!" He tousled the boy's hair. The kid nodded and gave Breen his cap pistols.

"STAY ON THE FLOOR UNTIL THIS IS OVER! YOU'LL BE SAFE HERE! LOCK YOUR DOORS!!"

The man nodded, the couple opened the two doors, crawled inside with the boy, and locked up as Manny ran back toward the van and took up a position several parked cars away.

Breen checked the cap guns, they were fully loaded. He darted into the street behind the arc of the FS firing at the police, waved his hands yelling "OVER HERE!," fired the cap guns at the enemy squad, then ran back behind the car. No response.

Breen ran into the street again, this time making sure he was seen by Fazio's soldiers, waved his arms and yelled, "HEY! OVER HERE!," pointed and fired the cap guns, then threw them at the nearest soldier.

The FS commander saw Manny and yelled to the soldier, "TAKE HIM OUT!" The soldier nodded, turned and fired a short burst, but Breen had vanished. The soldier ran over, stalked the cars parked on the north side of the street warily, crossed over to the sidewalk, and began checking under the automobiles, sticking his Pig under each car and firing blasts without looking.

He arrived at the car next to Breen.

From Manny's point of view under the car, he saw the legs of the soldier approach, saw the man bend down and thrust the weapon under the car he was hiding under.

Before he could discharge the weapon, Manny grabbed the barrel of the gun and yanked hard. Surprised, the combatant held on to the weapon and was pulled to the ground.

Breen rolled out from under the car and was on top of him in an instant, then aimed a powerful kick to his mid-section. When the soldier caved, Manny picked up his Pig and smashed his head in with the butt.

Manny felt an intense pain and looked at his right palm; it was already turning beet red from his contact with the barrel. Okay. Like everything else, it had to wait.

Breen took stock. His immediate problem had been solved. The dead soldier was wearing body armor, had an automatic weapon, and was wearing an eight grenade thigh-pouch with six fragmentation grenades and two M18 smoke grenades.

The Phoenix detective, retired Marine and karate champion fastened the grenade belt around his thigh, snapped on the armored vest, checked the Pig and its extra magazines, then peeked over the top of the car in time to see the cannon swivel toward the White House.

He needed a distraction.

Manny put the two smoke grenades on the hood of the car, stood up, pulled the pins, and tossed them one at a time on the street in front of the Howitzer. When they exploded, one emitted red smoke, the other yellow smoke that began obscuring the gunner's vision of the White House.

Adrenaline surged through him, a familiar burning sensation he likened to the shock from an electric current. It always saved him by infusing him with an extra reservoir of kinetic energy, surging power. Tremendous power. And a mental acuity that enabled him to adjust quickly to any emergency. Manny didn't know where it came from, but it was always there.

Staying in a crouched position, Breen carefully laid out the six remaining grenades on the hood. He could reach three targets: the right edge of the FS circle, the right center perimeter, and the soldier operating the 12.7mm machine gun on top of the Caesar.

Suddenly half a dozen Apache Gunships appeared over the White House and flew toward the Howitzer. Without warning, the two FS soldiers holding SA2 MANPADS each fired a surface-to-air missile, taking out two Apaches that exploded on the White House lawn.

Manny realized why the Apaches hadn't fired first: they were afraid of injuring civilians, women and children, still in the line of fire.

Sharon's Super Cobra flew in over the White House and settled down on the lawn.

Manny saw several men emerge; Sharon lifted off immediately and flew directly at the 155mm cannon, placing her Cobra between it and the Capitol.

Manny knew what she was doing. Sharon was willing to sacrifice her life to prevent the 155mm cannon from attacking the White House.

Thick smoke was obscuring the truck's target. Manny threw the first grenade at the machine gun post on the Caesar. While the missile was still airborne, he pulled the pin on the second grenade and threw it at the far right perimeter of the semi-circle of the FS, then pulled the third pin and launched the mag into the smoke where he estimated the middle of the FS's semi-circle should be.

Three explosions occurred almost simultaneously. Manny couldn't assess the damage due to the thick colored smoke. He grabbed one more grenade from his pouch, held his breath and ran through the swirling smog to the Caesar, climbed on top, and pulled the pin.

He yanked the cab door open, paused, then tossed the mag inside and jumped to the ground as the explosion inside the truck's cab ended the threat from the cannon. There was no more gunfire coming from the Fazio Squad.

He'd eliminated the threat to the White House … and to Sharon's Super Cobra.

Now he was ready for Vincent.

....

Breen ran toward 17th Street, cleared the smoke in time to see Fazio and J.J. extricate themselves from the wrecked BMW and run into The Ellipse, the park behind the White House.

As Manny approached the corner of 17th and Pennsylvania, a D.C. cop who'd survived by taking cover behind a tree, saw him coming, mistook him for the enemy, and began firing.

Manny dropped to the ground, saw it was a police officer and yelled, "I'M A COP! I'M A COP! I'M A COP! I'M A PHOENIX COP, DON'T SHOOT!"

"HOW DO I KNOW THAT?" the cop yelled back.

"THE TWO PERPS BEHIND THE ATTACK WERE IN THAT BMW! THEY'RE IN THE PARK! C'MON!"

Manny held his hands in the air, and continued running after Fazio and J.J. Confused, the cop hesitated, then decided to trust Manny and took off after him.

....

As they ran past the West Wing and entered the park, Fazio and J.J. both turned and fired. Manny dove to the ground, but the officer was too slow. He caught a round in the leg and went down. Manny started to turn back, but he waved Manny on.

"GO ON, GO ON! I'M ALL RIGHT!"

Manny nodded and took off after the two conspirators as J.J. tripped and fell. He recovered and fired at Breen who cut him down with a quick blast from the Pig, then ran past him after Fazio.

An Abrams Tank rumbled by, pushing Fazio's BMW in front of it.

Fazio ran toward The Ellipse followed by Manny a hundred feet behind. He fired at Breen, missing him. Manny tried to fire back, but was out of ammo.

Fazio stopped, then tossed a grenade at Manny who ducked behind a tree. The shock from the grenade stunned him and threw him to the ground.

As Fazio continued running across the park, Manny got to his knees, cleared his head, and followed.

The Boy scouts had been having a picnic in the Ellipse. There were nearly a hundred in attendance along with parents, grandparents, and friends. When they'd heard the gunfire, all had been herded to the safety of the White House by White House Security, leaving behind overturned tables, food, kegs of soft drinks, and personal belongings.

....

The Apache Gunships were hovering near the smoking van as Sharon's FBI chopper followed Manny into the park.

....

Dragging from exhaustion, Breen had closed on Fazio who was limping from the accident. Before Fazio could fire again, Manny dove in the air, tackled him, and knocked the .45 from his hands.

They went down together but Fazio threw Manny off, then jumped quickly to his feet. The ex-CIA operative was fresh and had the advantage. Manny got up slowly and stood facing him. Neither had a weapon.

The FBI chopper with Sharon inside was hovering overhead.

"You don't give up, do you?" Fazio said, taunting Breen.

Manny said nothing.

Fazio smiled. "That's because you're a cop.

Cops are stupid, they don't know when to stop."

Manny was slowly circling his enemy.

"By the way," Fazio continued, "too bad about your 'kid sister.'"

Manny lunged, Fazio easily evaded him and kicked Manny in the stomach. Manny went down.

"I have to warn you, little man ..." Fazio said, kicking Manny again ... "I was killing men before you were born .." He karate chopped Manny in the neck, Manny reeled.

"Not bad for a guy of 60," Fazio sneered.

"What's that? Your I.Q.?" Manny said, shaking his head to clear it.

Fazio smiled again, then hit Manny at a pressure point in his temple. Manny's eyes rolled back.

Fazio was circling Breen who was trying to get up. "You look tired, you should try going to bed."

Fazio landed on Manny's back with his knees. Manny groaned as Fazio pulled a two foot section of wire from his watch and wrapped it around Manny's neck, yanking Breen's head back off the ground. The instant the wire touched his throat, Breen instinctively took a deep breath.

Fazio leaned down close to Manny's ear and said intimately, "Was your sister a good fuck, Manny? Was she really a good *fuck!?*"

Fazio's comment was a fatal mistake. Manny's killer instinct swept through him like a tsunami. With a supreme effort, Breen got slowly to his knees and bucked his opponent over his head.

Fazio landed on the ground with Manny on top of him. Breen slammed his head repeatedly into Fazio's face as Fazio's nose split open, spurting blood.

As Fazio lay stunned, Manny struggled to his feet, then kicked Fazio in the ribs. When he tried a second kick, Fazio grabbed his foot and twisted him to the ground.

Manny rolled quickly, grabbed Fazio's watch from the grass and dove onto his back. He whipped the wire around Fazio's neck.

The CIA renegade's eyes widened as the wire tightened. He was seconds away from death when an MTVR screeched to a halt, a squad of Marines jumped out, and swiftly surrounded the combatants.

"Okay, knock it off!," the squad leader shouted.

Manny continued choking Fazio. The squad leader fired his M16 into the air. "YOU EAT THE NEXT ONE, MISTER!"

It got through to Manny, who loosened the wire and rolled over on the ground, exhausted, as Fazio started to regain his breath.

"I'm ... I'm Vincent Fazio, Sr., ... ex-CIA, ... here's my I.D., ..." Fazio said between gasps. He held his billfold up for the squad leader to see. "This man's a dangerous criminal .."

"*He's* the criminal," Manny said, "I'm Manny Breen, Phoenix P.D."

"Let's see your I.D." the squad leader demanded.

"I don't have it, it was —"

"LOOK OUT, HE'S GOT A GUN!" Fazio yelled as he grabbed his .45 from the ground and fired at Manny as the squad leader shot Fazio in the heart. Fazio looked surprised, stood for a moment. Then his eyes rolled back as he melted to the ground, dying on the way down.

....

Manny was on the ground with blood oozing from his shoulder from Fazio's bullet as a medic kneeled beside him. Sharon had landed the Cobra and was standing at Manny's side along with Baldwin and several FBI Agents.

"Is he going to be alright?" Sharon said to the medic.

The medic nodded. "Yeah, I'll patch him up, he'll be as bright as a penny."

Manny looked at Sharon. "You're one brave lady ..."

Sharon shrugged. "I just like to show off!"

Manny laughed.

....

Federal law enforcement officials and military personnel were everywhere. An EMS team wheeled J.J.'s body past the smoking hulk of the moving van and the bodies of Fazio's troops into an ambulance.

Manny and Sharon were searching for something on the street. Manny's shoulder and right hand were bandaged.

"Here they are!" Sharon said, picking up the two toy cap guns. She handed them to Manny.

"Thanks, I'll be right back."

Manny looked toward 17th Street NW and saw the parked car with the family still inside. He walked over, the man rolled the window down.

"Is it safe?" the man said. The little boy was sitting on his mother's lap in the passenger seat.

"Yes, it's definitely safe," Manny said with a smile. "I wanted to return these mighty pistols to their owner. What's his name?"

"John, after John Wayne."

Manny bent down and looked at the boy. "Well, John, you helped me get the bad guys today. Good job, pal!"

....

Washington Union Station in D.C.
9:00 a.m. Eastern Standard Time

Inside the Station on the departure track, Manny, his arm in a sling, was boarding an Amtrak for Phoenix with Sharon. He handed her a box of chocolates.

"For your habit."

Sharon took the gift and smiled. "Trying to make me fat?"

"You could use a few pounds. And by the way, you should get a Silver Star for what you did. Everyone's talking about it."

Sharon shrugged. "And you should get a Medal of Honor."

Manny smiled. "I already have one."

They boarded the train, and walked through the car until they came to a compartment.

"This is it," Sharon said.

Manny looked at the compartment and shook his head. "I can't go in there."

Sharon smiled and pushed him inside. "Some narrow, confined spaces can be very nice."

"Can we leave the door open?"

"Sure," Sharon said. In a few minutes, the train was picking up steam as Sharon stuck a "DO NOT

DISTURB" sign outside the sleeping berth and closed the door.

The End

To Receive a free copy of my Award-Winning Short Story, click the link below.

https://mailchi.mp/b8b59b4fbf52/httpsus17adminmailchimpcomlanding-pageseditid8379

Blurb: "Deathload"

When ex-CIA operative Vincent Fazio's son is killed by friendly fire in Desert Storm, Fazio takes revenge on the United States Air Force by building two monster trucks filled with Fuel Air bombs and chemical agents and sends them on a rampage across the United States. Their ultimate destination: The White House. When the trucks kill the sister of martial arts champion and Phoenix detective Manny Breen, Breen teams with Phoenix P.D. Department helicopter pilot Sharon Kramer in following and battling the two behemoths. Through many life-threatening experiences, the final battle moves to The White House for the final showdown between Breen and Vincent Fazio. A powerful narrative, a sensational ending.

Some URLs:

Cy's Website: https://www.cyyoungbooks.com-

Goodreads: https://www.goodreads.com/book/show/21702474-onions

Request For Reviews

Because reviews are the lifeblood of books, please consider leaving a few comments or a full review on Amazon and Goodreads after you read Deathload. It will be much appreciated and will go a long way in promoting this book to other potential readers. Thanks much.

Cy Young (Bio)

Mr. Young began his professional career as a member of the Meryl Abbot Dancers at the Empire Room of Chicago's Palmer House. After a year on the road dancing the "Steam Heat" number in *Pajama Game*, he repeated the performance in the New York City Center production. He appeared Off-Broadway in *The Boyfriend* and *Diversions* and a revue at New York's Blue Angel by *Chicago's* Fred Ebb. On Broadway, Cy was featured in a revue, *Girls Against The Boys* starring Bert Lahr, and was a principal in *Subways Are For Sleeping*, a Comden & Green musical. Simultaneously, he was a regular performer in revues at New York's elegant Upstairs At The Downstairs nightclub and can be heard on many *Upstairs* recordings. He is also a featured singer on Ben Bailey's *Painted Smiles* albums of Rodgers & Hart and Jerome Kern. Next came a national tour of *Once Upon a Mattress* in which he played Prince Dauntless to Buster Keaton's king, followed by a tour of *On A Clear Day* starring Howard Keel and Karen Black. Mr. Young stopped the show each night with a spectacular rendition of *Wait 'Til We're Six-*

ty Five. Called to London by *Diversions* director Steven Vinaver, he starred as Bobby in Sandy Wilson's *Divorce Me Darling* at the Globe Theatre and can be heard on the original cast album. Cy's most recent performances were in Oklahoma City's Lyric Theater's productions of *The Music Man* (Mayor Schinn) and *George M* (Jerry).

Mr. Young has had three plays published by Samuel French and three musicals produced in New York City Off-Broadway. Other writing credits include over 40 radio plays for Heartbeat Theatre in Los Angles, animation scripts for Rankin Bass, 2 optioned screenplays, and 3 children's musicals which he recently produced for performances in the New York Public School system. Cy's song, *Draw Me A Circle,* is on the *Barbra Streisand Third Album* and was used to open one of her early TV specials.

Mr. Young is a member of Actor's Equity Association, Screen Actor's Guild, and The American Federation of Television and Radio Artists. He holds an Active Membership in The Dramatists Guild as well as The Author's League of America and is a graduate of Northwestern University.

Reviews

Below find a review from a fellow writer from the Kyle Writer's Forum:

Deathload--You won't be able to stop reading!
A review by Christine Reid

Hang onto your hat because Deathload is here and it's taking you along for the most breathtaking ride of your life. Phoenix detective Manny Breen has the mind and muscle to deal with whatever comes his way. A former Marine who served during the Gulf War, Breen, as a young man, was a karate champion and kickboxer who was known for his speed and power. He is going to need plenty of both when he comes up against Vincent Fazio, Sr., an incredibly wealthy and twisted man who is determined to wreak vengeance on the military for the loss of his son during Desert Storm. The story revs up right away as Manny is drawn into a terrifying, white-knuckled ride down an Arizona freeway, following two driverless, hulking, black trucks that each seem to have a mind of their own, with high-tech weaponry and a seemingly impenetrable structure. The trucks are being closely tracked by Fazio and his gang of goons who are determined to follow their boss' orders, no matter how outrageous. Through vivid detail, the reader can see the violent attacks against the military that Fazio orchestrates and can feel Manny's intense, controlled anger and determination to stop this madman. Helping Manny is the smart and sassy Sharon Kramer who knows her way around choppers. Also a Gulf War veteran, Sharon feels drawn to the complicated Manny and does her best to keep up with the explosions, collisions and quickly changing conditions, all while deftly piloting a helicopter. The action-packed story will keep you hooked until the end, when you can finally get your breath back. Deathload contains page after page of excitement as well as characters that you won't ever be able to forget.

....

Also, a review from Don Sloan of Midwest Review:

Deathload Review

Two enormous black 18-wheelers take on a deadly life of their own in this heart-stopping thriller by superb storyteller Cy Young.

The driverless big rigs first make an appearance on Interstate 10 outside Tucson, Arizona, where, traveling at dangerously high speeds, they force driver Betsy Breen off the road, causing her car to burst into flames and killing the young woman instantly.

Without even slowing down, the trucks race out of sight down the featureless interstate, leaving Tucson Police Detective Manny Breen -- Betsy's brother -- in shock, staring down the embankment and watching his younger sister die a fiery, senseless death.

But that's just the beginning of a carefully calculated killing campaign that will result in the deaths of tens of thousands within 48 hours. Because these are no ordinary trucks, even given their ability to cruise the nation's highways at 100+ mph -- without benefit of a human behind the wheel.

They have been created solely to extract revenge for the death of one man's son in the first Gulf War. Marine Lance Corporal Vincent Fazio Jr. was killed in a friendly fire incident. And now his billionaire father has armed these state-of-the-art big rigs with a frightening arsenal of weapons of mass destruction to decimate the entire population of six U.S. Air Force bases -- along with the White House in Washington D.C.

Detective Breen steps up to the challenge of finding and neutralizing the trucks. And he has help from a colorful supporting cast of law enforcement personnel, including a special bond with Phoenix police helicopter pilot Sharon Kramer.

But it's Breen who must often go it alone against these powerful and devastating juggernauts. They try repeatedly to kill him in some of the most cinematic sequences we've seen. Indeed, readers will be eagerly looking for the tag line: "Soon to be a major motion picture."

We award our very highest rating of five-plus stars to this excellent foray into the crowded genre of vivid action/adventure books.

But this one is elevated far above the rest for a storyline that serves up much more than just high octane action. Real characters come to life on these pages and force you to care deeply about whether they survive. Many don't.

But the ones who do will stay with you long after you've finished the final chapter. And you'll be eagerly awaiting a sequel, starring one of Hollywood's most popular action movie mainstays. Who will that be? Stay tuned.

....

And a final review from Marine SSGT Carlos Garcia, Recruiter for San Marcos

Hello sir,

After reading your book, it has a lot of life-like characteristics. The vehicles used in the book, the life style of Marines, and how we carry ourselves, it's very convincing. I would say this book is very well put together. I like how you did your research to make the person feel what it's like to be in the story and how everything matches in the Marine protocol.

I recommend this to all readers out there for intense action.

****

PLEASE SHARE WITH YOUR FRIENDS! WRITE A REVIEW! POST ON FACEBOOK! If you want to read a **free copy** from my file of "Deathload," email me at: cy.young.jr@austin.r-r.com, or send a request via my website at cyy-oungbooks.com.

....

Deathload Trailer
https://youtu.be/VUx3qH23UR0

Offer of Free Published Short Story -
https://mailchi.mp/b8b59b4fbf52/http-sus17adminmailchimpcomlanding-pagesedi-tid8379

Made in the USA
San Bernardino, CA
30 June 2019